SEVEN ACTS OF BETRAYAL

A Murder in Cape Cod

A Kyra Stevens Book 1

Cynthia Brenner

Seven Acts of Betrayal is a work of fiction. Names, characters, places and incidents
are the product of the author's imagination or are used fictitiously. Any resemblance
to actual events, locals, or persons living or dead, is entirely coincidental.

ISBN 13: 978-0692377604
ISBN 10: 0692377603

www.cynthia@ccbrenner.com

ACKNOWLEDGMENTS

I discovered that writing a book is only the beginning and that I owe a debt of gratitude to everyone along the way who helped and encouraged me.

The Hudson Valley Chapter of RWA

Michelle Rosario and Beverly Oberst

My first reader Jules Balbert who read every word and suggested some of his own.

And my computer guru Owen Balbert.

VISIT: WWW.cynthia@ccbrenner.com

VISIT: WWW.kyra.stevens@ccbrenner.com

TABLE OF CONTENTS

CHAPTER ONE

*S*he stood in the middle of the Airport's high-end car rentals stuffing her luggage into a white SUV. A redheaded good-looking bitch that wouldn't look at him twice. She paused for a moment shielding her eyes from the sun and watched a departing jet.

He made a quick comparison to the photo on his cellphone. It was definitely her!

He could smell the money. Pictured what it would bring. One hundred thousand dollars was more than he had earned on any other hit.

A few more minutes and his wait would be over. He'd make the phone call, the payment would be wired and the money his.

The woman stopped admiring the plane. She finished loading the car and closed the trunk. Quickly, she moved to the driver's door.

"Now or never," he shouted. "Here comes the dough, Baby." He jammed his foot on the pedal and barreled straight at her.

Some daft woman yelled and waved her arms. The redhead disappeared from sight while several Airport Security shouted and ran toward his car.

"Damn!" He zoomed across the lot swerved onto the ramp punching the steering wheel over and over with a fist. "Damn! Damn!"

———※※———

Kyra Stevens had expected cobwebs and dust in the beach front estate loaned to her for three months, not a dead body in the dining room.

She glanced at her watch, two hours since she phoned the police. How much longer would she have to wait to be questioned? She thought of her itinerary and the unexpected time she had lost.

She stared across the hallway watching the Medical Examiner hover around the murdered woman. She could see his lips move as he spoke to the homicide Lieutenant, but his voice was low and didn't carry over the buzz from the room filled with investigators.

After Lieutenant Braden had arrived, and walked past with the briefest of introductions, the others blatantly ignored her. Steadfast, they worked their jobs.

Each time the front doors opened blustery March winds whipped into the sprawling mansion chilling her bones. She drummed manicured nails on the arm of the oversized wing chair and burrowed into the collar of her denim jacket—waiting for him to talk to her.

The Lieutenant was tall with a rigid set to his broad shoulders. He tilted aviator sunglasses up onto black, wavy hair, and squatted; examining something on the body the M.E. pointed too. In one quick movement, he glanced in her direction, then back to the dead woman. His deep sun-tanned face so handsome she thought her heart would stop at the impact.

The two men stood. Annoyance creased Braden's face. Every few moments, he turned, eyes riveted on her.

What did he have to be annoyed about? He and his crew were in her way—delaying her schedule. She was the one who had to bring a billion dollar venture to the table before June. Her boss, James Enrico expected nothing less. That's how she climbed the corporate ladder. Delivering what was assigned. That's why she stood on the fourth rung from the top not letting another get in her way.

Behind the men, the dining room table was long enough for two dozen guests. It held a clutter of china, glassware and knick-knacks and looked like a display in one of the flea markets back in Florida. Except, here the layer of dust was so thick she could have written her initials in it.

But cleaning the dust and tackling JE's new project was now the least of her problems. A lot more was on the line in this island paradise. Her insides clenched. Definitely, more to lose, maybe her life!

Kyra's attention returned to the body sprawled across the Oriental rug. She wondered how long it would take someone to notice the victim had red hair like hers— and that both of them were about the same height and size. Enough similarities to crawl under her skin, and she blurted, "Maybe the killer thought she was me." The words flew out of her mouth, a childhood habit still carried with her. She sucked in a deep breath, wished she could pull them back, but it was too late.

The Lieutenant was heading towards her and seemed to overhear. His brow arched in surprise, his long legs crossed the entrance hall in two strides. In one swift movement, he pulled over a side chair and sat facing her.

Eyes, green as rain—drenched leaves stared into hers, a nerve beat above his right jawline. "Who on the Cape doesn't want you around?" His deep timbered voice vibrated in the high—vaulted rooms. Heads turned.

"Don't know. I've never been in Massachusetts before."

"It is an odd thing to say that someone wants to kill you." He flicked the corner of the business card she gave earlier to the Whales Bay police officer and read aloud, "Kyra Stevens, Executive Vice President of Acquisitions: Harbor Lights Hotels, Miami, Florida." His eyes probed—studying her face. "A long way off."

"Three and a half hours to Boston without layovers," Kyra paused. "How did the poor woman die?"

"She was stabbed."

"So much blood." Kyra shivered in the chilled, dusty room. "What was she doing in the house?"

"I hoped you could tell me."

"No idea." She shook her head. "My plane landed this morning. I picked up my rental and drove down from Logan Airport."

"You never said why."

"Why?"

"Someone would want to kill you."

Kyra glanced around, swallowed hard. Too soon to say too much. If this murder had nothing to do with her, why let the Lieutenant in on her personal life. It would confuse his investigation and give her hurdles to jump.

After all, Cape Cod was over sixteen hundred miles away from James Enrico's Miami Beach flagship hotel and the first dead woman. How could the two murders be related, anyway?

The Lieutenant's penetrating eyes stayed level with hers. Their intensity shook her. She felt her cheeks burn and she heard herself falter. "It's just the resemblance; same hair color, about my size. I was upset. Silly of me, but I am tired. It's been a long day and I worked for most of the flight."

She'd spent half of the trip from Miami to Boston on the laptop preparing for her so-called vacation—slash—business trip. However, her things—to—do—list did not include discovering a dead woman, calling the police and watching them analyze the crime scene.

A day's set—back, James Enrico would say.

Braden gave a wintry smile. She doubted he believed her. His problem.

Her problem; not to lose track of the reason she was in Massachusetts.

"Officer Pirro said you're not the owner. Are you renting?"

"Harbor Lights owns the property. The CEO loaned it to me." Her gaze locked with his. "Until June!"

"Vacation?"

"A little vacation, a little business." She gave her best-disinterested smile.

What James Enrico had actually said was who could be as lucky as her? Having a boss who gave perks like an ocean front mansion and a three-month vacation. JE ignoring the fact that she had to put together the venture for a billion dollar resort in the same timeframe. And that most of the area's residents would be against it.

They usually were.

She wondered where the hot Lieutenant would stand on the issue of swooping up a million dollars worth of virgin beachfront property and turning it into a glitzy panoramic resort.

He seemed amused by her answer. A hint of a smile toyed at the corners of a full and sensual mouth, but his eyes were humorless. Perhaps, he had seen too many murders in his job. Though she thought, just the opposite existed on the Cape.

He looked like the young side of forty. Didn't wear a wedding ring. He had square, straight nails and long fingers. She had to admit, this man was a presence.

"What time did you arrive?" the Lieutenant asked.

"About noon."

"See anyone?"

"No."

"A car? Delivery van?"

"There was a silver SUV in the driveway."

"Explain what happened when you got here? Was the door open—closed?"

"I got out of the car. Unlocked the front door."

"You're positive it was locked?"

"Absolutely."

"And the security system?"

"It wasn't set." She took a deep breath. "I didn't have to enter the access code. I turned the key, opened the door, and shouted hello..."

"Why? Whom were you expecting?"

"The housekeeper, Mrs. Nelson, comes in when there are guests. To put things in order. Just before I left Miami, her daughter had an emergency. I wasn't sure when Mrs. Nelson was returning. Anyway, it's big, empty—a strange house."

Cold and wind-swept, she added to herself. A house built for families, lots of friends, not the work-alcoholic right hand to a business legend like James Enrico.

"Okay, then what?" the Lieutenant persisted.

"I turned toward the dining room, saw the body…I think I screamed." She heard a rasp catch in her throat. She slumped back in the chair—hungry, thirsty and tired. This never—ending day had the potential of turning into a never—ending night.

She bent down rummaged in her tote. She needed a moment to collect her thoughts.

"Can I help?"

"I was looking for my bottle of water."

"No problem. I'll get one." In a couple of strides, he was gone.

What was the man up too? Seeking more info to question her about. Kyra cleared her throat. And what would JE say when she called with today's bit of news?

Bad timing for her to get a lawyer!

Her eyes drifted to the wrap—around glass walls. The view made her feel as if the diamond tipped waters of Nantucket Sound sat like a private swimming hole outside the French doors. JE's clapboard and flagstone three story appeared haunted and ill—kempt. Her Miami condo in tip—top shape overlooked the Inter-Coastal and could fit into the mansion's living room where she sat.

Braden was back. He removed the top, offered his bottle of water, sat down, and this time took out a pen and small notebook.

Beware of gifts. The phrase tumbled through her mind as she drank.

He checked off a few items, and then with a quizzical expression, asked, "Did you notice the victim's pocketbook or an attaché case?"

"Pocketbook...?" her voice trailed off. "No."

"And the keys? Where did you get them?"

"Where? Mr. Cassel gave them to me before I left Florida."

"Who?"

"James Enrico Cassel, President and Chairman of Harbors Board of Directors."

"JEC Industries?" His eyes widened.

"Yes." The itch was back. Her gut tightened. She steeled against the rush of questions her job and her boss generated.

"What kind of business?" Suspicion dusted his words.

"I beg your pardon." Not sure what he was asking, she needed to be precise.

"You said a little vacation, a little business?"

"H'mm... Confidential."

Braden frowned, gritted his teeth.

She knew she hit a nerve.

Kyra put the bottle of water on the side table, opened her palm wide, a slight shrug. She smiled, like one professional to another. Her stomach muscles cramped. A surge of helplessness ran through her. Imperative, she stayed focused. Her job demanded it. Her career taught do not show emotion, play it cool. She had to come out of this smelling like a rose to maintain her influence with the corporate board.

He leaned in towards her. "But are you planning to do business on the cape, or relax on an extended vacation?"

"Oh no." Not really, she told herself. Even JE had weighed the odds of pulling—off a low-rise resort and golf emporium in the midst of the quaint, quiet dunes. "Maybe a meeting or two. Reaffirm my contacts. Otherwise, I'd like to do some local sight—seeing."

"But even if you did, you wouldn't say."

Kyra laughed out loud. Cutting through the police jargon and buzz, her laughter made heads turn.

"Could the victim have been here for one of your meetings?"

"Lieutenant—please, give me a chance to catch my breath." She gave a nervous laugh in spite of herself. "A meeting? I haven't even strolled on your beautiful beaches."

"The sunrises are the best time."

"Perfect. That's when I plan my day and have a coffee."

"Ah. I've caught it."

"What?"

"The Virginias? Or the Carolinas? You've a trace of a southern accent. Where are you from?"

"North Carolina." She swallowed hard, licked her lips.

"I thought fast—track people had everything set—up before they boarded the plane."

"Remember, fifty, fifty."

"I know. A little vacation and a little business." His smile toyed once again near the corners of his mouth. Then he was off on another tangent. "Which phone did you use to call the police?"

"My cell, of course."

"I need the number."

"It's on my card." She nodded toward his hand.

Quickly glancing at it, he tucked the card in his breast pocket and asked, "Then what?"

Kyra had the instinctive feeling she had just become Braden's number one object of attention. At least, until he had the redheaded lady's murderer in his clutches. She felt it would be wise to distance herself from him.

"I was told to wait in the courtyard. I did."

"That's it?" His eyes darkened and he tucked the small notepad and pen inside his pocket next to her card. As he moved, she saw his gun clipped to his belt. Man on the move; an advertisement for danger.

"I came back into the house with Officer Pirro," she offered. What other answers was he looking for?

"When did you touch the body?"

"I didn't."

Braden didn't ask if she had. He presumed.

What did she miss?

"There's blood on the sole of your sneaker," he said, as if reading her mind.

He probably could—the way he locked into her eyes.

Her heartbeat quickened. "The dining room is soaked with blood," she stated in a solemn tone.

"But if you stood in the hallway and didn't enter, how did the blood get on your sneaker?"

"After I called..." her voice trailed off. As nervous as his questions made her, she knew she should tell it, as it happened. It had worked for her in Miami. Here on the Cape, she was alone without James Enrico and Harbors' battery of lawyers. Her choices limited. She had to stay within the truth. "When I called 911, they asked so many questions. I thought I should take a better look at..."

"The victim," Braden finished the sentence for her. "You felt for a pulse?"

"Why would I do that? I'm not a medical person. Wouldn't know how..." her voice trembled. "I tried to help. Phoned as soon as I found her." She leaned forward, wanted him to understand. "I never saw so much blood in my life. She was dead wasn't she, before I arrived?"

"Yes." He clasped his hands between his knees. "Her throat was slashed—ear to ear and then numerous times on her body."

Kyra closed her eyes to stop the buzzing in her head, the swaying of the floor. Who was the stabbing meant for? And why? "Oh, dear God! I didn't touch her."

"Someone did."

9

"Ask the murderer," she muttered between clenched teeth. I didn't do anything wrong."

The Lieutenant looked like someone kicked him below the belt. Once again, annoyance crossed his face and glistened in those green eyes. "You discovered the body and lied about entering the crime scene."

"That makes me—what—a killer?"

"I didn't say that, but right now, you're all we have."

"You can't be serious?"

Kyra scrambled out of the chair, nauseated that someone thought she was capable of committing such a horrific act. "Did you want me to ignore she was lying there? Not phone the police? Run out?"

Several officers poked their heads into the room.

"Miss Stevens…". Lieutenant Braden stood. His eyes glued to her every move. "Mam…"

"Perhaps, I should have stepped over her and left? I thought I was doing the right thing." She paced the parquet floor, arms wrapped under her breasts. Whirling about, she stopped dead center in front of the windows, opened her hands wide. Seething, she hissed. "When are your people leaving? This is my home, for the next couple of months, anyway." She hugged herself. "Who—who cleans up the blood?"

From across the room, Tom Braden stared at his chief suspect. Eyes—almond shaped and azure blue as the Bay behind her—blazed with anger. The late afternoon sun turned her hair aflame. His gut twisted. Kyra had two things that fit the profile of most violent killers, fury and a short fuse. And right now, both were directed at him.

He heard the anger in her voice. Tried not to show a reaction on his part. He understood that at times the sight of blood or a dead body could put a person on the defensive. But his gut told him Kyra was holding something back. He had to know what.

As a New York City Homicide detective, he had seen a lot of murders. But after the death of his wife, Ivy, in an automobile accident, he hadn't thought another dead body could affect him. He was so wrong.

It had taken a couple of years after the accident to find this position, a Lieutenant heading the new Massachusetts State Homicide Commission covering the entire Cape and the surrounding area.

He had jumped at the opportunity. He submitted his papers, relocated and left New York City. Today, seeing the blood and savagery, the old horrific feelings of what people can do to one another returned.

His one and only anchor, Matt, pulled the strings to his heart. Sometimes when his seven year old tilted his head, or drew with chalk on the driveway, Tom could see Ivy in his son's art and his movements. His heart ached that she could not. But his son was healthy and happy; and Tom felt he did the smart thing in moving to Cape Cod.

Kyra's pale complexion turned white like the pristine beach as the emergency workers removed the body. Her narrow shoulders sloped and she shivered. Turning, her gaze shifted to the diamond tipped waves crashing against the low sea wall.

She was a knock—out, long—legged, deep breasted, thick wavy hair. She came up to his chin in her sneakers, maybe five foot six. A smattering of freckles across her nose told him she didn't frequent Miami Beaches. Too busy working, he supposed. What kind of social life did she have? Maybe, it wasn't much better than his.

"Are you okay?" Tom walked up to her and set his hand on her shoulder.

"Yes," Kyra said.

She didn't seem to notice he was alive. She had come alone flying across ten states, determined to achieve. Didn't wear a ring, but what was James Enrico to her? She was young—he thought early thirties—had a prominent position in a national corporation. He knew her profile without even reading her resume; smart, competent, goal—oriented, determined to climb higher and higher.

He had stopped—gotten off the one—way escalator and settled in. But he hadn't stopped doing his job.

He was damn good at that, and needed answers, quickly. But until the Lab and the M.E got back to him, all he had was Kyra Stevens from Miami, Florida.

"Could the murder be a case of mistaken identity?" Tom asked.

Kyra shrugged her shoulders.

"It's important we discuss it. Not shrug it off." Would she see he'd rather she was a potential victim and not a suspect? Though she might not appreciate that, either. Tom bit his lip to keep from smiling.

"I told you, I was tired."

"But you still thought the victim looked like you?"

"The words popped out of my mouth."

"I find it hard to believe that someone in your position blurts things out." His voice rose in anger. "Who has a motive?"

"No one, I can think of," her tone matched his.

"We'll need a day, perhaps two, to search the house and the grounds. And I'd like Mrs. Nelson's phone number."

"Of course. It's in my cell." Kyra crossed the room.

He couldn't take his eyes from the sway of her rounded hips in the designer jeans. A little kernel of hope nudged that she was tired from lack of sleep and more than a bit hungry. She'd welcome a sign of friendship. He had to keep tabs on her. She could take off in a moment and fly back to where she came from.

"I know a nice bed and breakfast. They can put you up for a couple of nights. It's quiet this time of year."

"I guess I don't have a choice."

"Suppose not."

"Thank you, then. I couldn't bear to sleep with the blood."

"There's a little café about a half mile down the road from the B&B where you can grab a bite. Oh, and one other thing."

"What?" Her eyes narrowed.

"I need your sneakers."

"My sneakers?"

"They're evidence. We have to test the blood."

She shot a poisonous glance straight at him before reaching into her tote and pulling out a set of tagged car keys. "I have a change in my carry—on."

She made a move toward the doorway, but before she took a second step, he called out, "Wait! Don't walk in them. Where is your luggage? I'll send an officer."

"In the trunk." Her face was open, yet sad. Like she caught a new glimpse of what he was thinking—but not the entire picture, and she worried.

"Tell the officer to unzip the blue duffel. There's a pair of black flats on top." She handed the Lieutenant the keys and sat down unlacing her sneakers.

And realized, she had never mentioned she was almost run down at the airport. She couldn't help but wonder if the car had hit her, would the dead woman in the dining room still be alive?

CHAPTER TWO

The Lieutenant's directions to the B&B were easy to follow and the drive took Kyra less than fifteen minutes. The Inn was bright and clean, her room large and comfortable. The owner helped with the luggage and recommended the same Café as the Lieutenant.

But Kyra drove in circles until she saw the hanging sign swaying in the soft evening breeze.

Barney's was at the intersection of two country lanes over-looking a marina. Dusk was already falling as she pulled into the Café's parking lot. Delicious aromas of grilled fish and meat, baked pies and sweets made her mouth water, and she quickened her pace walking toward the grey-shingled building. She realized outside of several bottles of water, she hadn't eaten since her morning coffee and muffin.

Inside, the restaurant was burnished mahogany, hurricane lamps and ship steering wheels. A tall, young woman met her in the entranceway. "Good evening, I'm Diane. I'll be your server tonight."

Kyra looked around the half—filled restaurant that had a magnificent view of the ocean. "I'd like a window table." She nodded toward the rear of the room that overlooked the dock.

The waitress led her to one, put down a menu and took her drink order.

Kyra leaned back, eyes half closed, gazed out across the horizon trying to clear her head. The sun was lowering into the sea. Most of the boats were in dry dock. Just the opposite from this time of year in Miami!

The waitress placed a glass of wine and a breadbasket in front of her and asked, "Ready to order?"

"Yes," Kyra flipped the menu open.

"Bouillabaisse! It's awesome." The Lieutenant's voice rang out as he walked toward her.

"Oh," the server gasped. "She didn't say you were together. I would have given her your table." The young woman's disappointment was almost palpable.

"Not a big deal," Tom said as he pulled out a chair. "May I?" He sat down not waiting for an answer. "Try it. The best bouillabaisse on the Cape."

"I will." Kyra smiled while her gut knotted. After her day, she was looking forward to a quiet meal, and did not anticipate spending one minute more with the Lieutenant.

Was this why he recommended the restaurant, so he could walk in on her? Perhaps, discuss her sneakers marked with blood. He wasn't fooling anyone. He knew the blood was the victim's.

"Two dinners," Tom said, returning the menus to the waitress who eyed Kyra up and down before sauntering away.

"I think she likes—admires—you." Kyra unfolded the white napkin cradled in the breadbasket and took a piece of flat bread.

"I eat here several times a week," Tom said.

"Don't cook?" She pushed the basket towards him.

"My hours." He frowned. "Makes it hard—the shopping, preparing."

A grin broke across his face and he started to get up. Kyra turned in her chair. A tall, barrel chested man was moving quickly towards them. Both men hugged each other.

"Doesn't matter how many dead bodies turn up, you're in safe hands with our Tommy."

"My brother—in—law, Barney," Tom said with a chuckle. "Kyra Stevens. She's moving into the Cassel place for a couple of months."

"Are you the one who found the body?" He reached across offering his hand. Soft grey eyes studied her face. Grey hairs streaked his blond ponytail and she caught a broad Bostonian accent.

"I'm sorry to say I was."

"Well, we won't hold it against you. It'll just give us something to talk about until we learn more about you."

Kyra wasn't sure if she should laugh, or not, and wondered who were the We? She looked from one to the other, but the two men were on to other things.

"The Town Board is already getting antsy. It'll be great, if you solve the case before the weather gets warmer and the season starts."

Tom chuckled. "Depends when spring blows in this year. It's only the beginning of March."

"But you don't have the board members calling every half hour. Murder is a killer."

"Like I always tell you, don't pick up the phone. Use Caller ID. It really works. And as soon as I have a solid case, I'll proceed to the DA and let you know."

For a brief second, Barney studied the Lieutenant. Then tilting his head, he said. "A pleasure to meet you, Ms. Stevens. Come back soon. With or without the big guy. But he'd be smart to bring you." Barney took off before she could say a word.

She felt her cheeks burn and swore the Lieutenant was blushing. "News travels fast," she murmured, lowering her eyes and taking a sip of wine. "Guess they expect the murder solved just as quick."

"Professional concern. Can't blame them." Tom leaned back, his tone taut. "The Cape is a resort area, the backbone of everyone's livelihood. Crime is bad for business." He nodded at Barney's retreating back. "Third generation restaurant owner—par excellence—and Whales Bay Mayor."

"Sounds like you have pressure from the job as well as from family. I know the feeling."

"It happens." He shrugged.

"And Barney?"

"Works his ass off between this town and the restaurant."

She quirked an eyebrow.

"He's my sister's husband," Tom said thinking, thank God, for Rory. She was his mainstay when it came to his son.

"Personally, I haven't had a day off all year. I know how it feels." She gave an ingratiating smile wide and open.

Perfect teeth all in a row; shiny white pearls. Cool it Braden. You sound like a poet. They're just teeth. And this wasn't a date. They were just two stray people having a meal, or a police lieutenant who was putting in a little overtime with a possible suspect.

"You don't cook, you eat out, probably bring in lots of take out." Kyra buttered her bread. "Tell you what I can do." She took a second sip of wine, and bit off a piece of bread, chewed with deliberation and swallowed. "Considering that I'm an unwilling participant in this murder, I'd like to know how the case proceeds and how it ends. Keep me in the loop and I'll cook dinner for you once I get back into the house."

Tom choked, cleared his throat and took a drink of water. "The lady has time to cook?" Was all he could manage?

Kyra gave a drop—dead look, followed by a teasing smile. "Nouveau cuisine."

"Southern style or Continental?" What was she really after and why? Chief of Police Williams would have hauled her in as a suspect, if he had heard her offer.

"Either." Kyra waved one hand wide. "Probably will take several dinners. Don't you agree? I mean it's not like you have DNA and eyewitnesses lined up in a row to identify the killer."

"Could be happening as we speak." He chuckled, sliced off an end of the home baked bread. One spunky babe! Maybe she was coming on to him?

He should be so lucky.

"So, is it a deal maker?" She reached across the table to shake hands. Her gaze, direct and innocent—held his.

Instincts told him don't promise what you can't deliver. But at this very moment, in this very place, the little Kyra offered was too much to ignore.

"A deal." He shook her hand. Soft skin, slender delicate fingers felt lost within his grasp. For the briefest of seconds, Tom didn't leave go. What if she was cleared as a suspect? Then could he hold her? Would she be able to ignore he was a cop? A romantic interlude they both could look back on. In your dreams, Braden!

The waitress placed their food in front of them.

Kyra fanned the napkin across her lap, uncovered her tureen and inhaled the aromas now floating free into the air. "Did you learn who the woman was?" she asked after a deep breath.

Tom speared a shrimp. "I'm not counting this meal as one of your home—cooked dinners."

"Oh."

He swore she pouted.

"If you prefer to recite a litany in one shot—and not share tidbits as they arise, that's your call?" She popped a chunk of lobster into her mouth.

Give a little! Take a little! This lady was one excellent game player. "You made your point. The dead woman's name is Megan Polk. Familiar?"

"No."

"She was probably in your house by a fluke."

"What do you mean?" She stiffened, stared across the table.

If she held her fork any tighter, it would leave indents on her skin. "The victim was a real estate broker, had an appointment to see..."

"Not the Cassel place," Kyra interjected, frowning.

"That's correct. She was supposed to be at the Sullivan Compound next door. They're traveling this season and would like to rent. Megan is new to the job. Either she went to the wrong address, or wanted to take a better look at the Sullivan's neighbors."

"How awful. Family?"

"Separated about six months. No children. Her parents winter in Florida. Just spoke to them. They're flying up tomorrow. Isn't that where you're from?" He downed a quarter of his Samuel Adams, picked up on the tension spreading between them. Not the way he wanted the evening to go. He hadn't even touched her and his chest felt tight. But he was a cop and couldn't stop himself from cross-examining.

Her mouth settled in a thin line. "Almost everyone's parents go down to Florida, a good percentage from New England. Cold winters in these parts." She ignored his question, moved on to her own. "And you?" she asked jabbing into the tureen.

"Me?"

"Where are you from? You don't sound like a native."

"New York—born and bred."

"Ah, the big city."

"Each has its good and bad."

"Spoken like an ex—city cop." Strain creased her brow.

Once again, she was becoming uptight, couldn't seem to relax. More than likely, the first time she interfaced with a homicide detective. Her reaction was typical.

"You're not with the Whales Bay Police Department?" she pressed. Her need to know seemed to overcome her reluctance to his occupation.

"No. I'm with the State's Homicide Division. I cover Cape Cod and the surrounding areas on the mainland."

"Then you handle a lot of murder cases?"

"Not as much as I did in Manhattan. This is Whales Bay's first big one since 2008."

Surprise creased her brow.

"But other towns had more than their share," he added. "Keeps me busy."

She hesitated, propped her fork on the plate. "Are we getting to know one another, or asking trick questions?"

She faced him squarely, didn't pull her punches. And she was so beautiful he wanted all of it. What was wrong with that? He couldn't overstep his boundaries, and knew solving the case meant she wouldn't be around for long.

"It would be nice to do both." He couldn't believe he said it.

"H'mm." Her face colored pink, but her tone softened. "I...I never saw so much blood in all my life. Do you know how many times she was stabbed?"

"The M.E. has yet to determine that."

"And the weapon?"

"Haven't found it," he paused. "I'm asking you to think about what you said earlier. That the killer mistook the victim for you."

"That was nerves. When I saw that her hair color was the same as mine. But the idea is ridiculous, I just arrived in Massachusetts today."

"Who knew?" he prompted.

"Not anyone who'd want to kill me." Her voice sounded uneven. "Maybe Megan was attacked by someone she knew? A rendezvous gone bad."

"And the killer murdered her in lieu of sex?" Tom stared incredulously across the table. The ME had raised the same possibility.

"Some men can't take rejection."

CHAPTER THREE

Later that night, Kyra lay back against the pillows in the large front room of the bed and breakfast. She'd tried to stop reliving her first day on the Cape, but as a warped video, the events played over and over in her mind.

Barely able to keep her eyes open, and yet unable to sleep, her thoughts turned to the Lieutenant. He seemed to be very knowledgeable in his field and she wondered why he relocated to the Cape. Quite obvious, there was more to Braden than met the eye. Tom—he had said. A solid name! A solid guy! A hottie.

And then there was James Enrico, who wasn't happy to hear her narrative of the day's happenings. Didn't she remember he had scheduled a board meeting for the first thing tomorrow morning and had planned to turn in early?

He growled that she woke him. Growled about the dead woman on his dining room carpet, and even growled about Lieutenant Braden heading the investigation. The CEO unreasonably annoyed that Braden was in charge of the Cape's Homicide Division. He worried that a Massachusetts State Police Lieutenant specializing in murder cases might know about the first woman killed in his Miami flagship hotel.

JE speculating he might be dragged into this latest case. The notoriety would be disastrous for someone in his position.

Kyra clutched the phone so tight, her nails left imprints in her palm.

Nothing she said assured him. She reiterated that states don't track each other's murders especially a year old killing over sixteen hundred miles away. Local police concentrated on their own cases and were too busy to go cross-country.

But James Enrico persisted. Had she forgotten about Social Networking and the FBI?

Before she could respond, he had growled again. "It is imperative that this Braden person keeps you in the loop. How will you make this happen?"

"I've already handled it. I'm playing Rachel Ray."

"H'mm," JE murmured in a pill and liquor-induced tone, "And what about Biloxi?"

"Biloxi," she had gasped? "What about it?"

James Enrico's voice froze. Silence as cold as slivers of ice snaked through the phone lines.

"You're not going to tell me what happened?"

James Enrico's tone flat lined, as if it was uttered from the dead. "You've enough on your plate, Kyrita."

Chills crept up her spine. Cramps shot through her stomach almost doubling her over. Was someone else killed in Biloxi? Harbors didn't have a hotel there. Was a new one planned? Hidden—from her, the fourth—in—command. She felt like a hornet's nest just exploded on top of her head. She was only gone one day.

"A great report, Kyrita. As usual, you're the one I count on. Stay on target. Buena's noches." JE clicked off.

Now, she listened to the wind rustling through the trees, the woods crackling with the calls of night animals and birds. Not a car drove by. She didn't know if the blackness outside her windows belonged to the meeting of ocean and sky, or a deserted landscape made—up of unoccupied vacation homes and early—to—bed residents. The eeriness was enough to make her heartbeat race at the absolute desolation of her surroundings.

She yearned for the familiarity and warmth of her home. Longed to return. She recalled The Outer Banks where she grew up, so long ago. Maybe she'd call. Maybe she could grab a few days, fly down and see her parents.

Still not able to call it a night, she reached for the cell phone, and punched in the last speed code she'd entered before leaving Miami. She huddled under the patchwork quilt, the phone pressed to her ear.

"Hello!" The voice was cold.

"Lawrence! Kyra Stevens."

"Your trip went well?" the real estate attorney asked dryly. No change in tone even after all their business calls and e-mails. He too, sounded annoyed that she had phoned. Obviously, the Boston media where he lived still hadn't honed in on the redhead's murder.

"Yes," she responded.

Actually, it was her arrival on the Cape that hadn't gone well, not the trip, she theorized.

"I looked at my schedule," she continued. "Wednesday would be fine. How about a working lunch? The mansion has a glorious view and the place is quiet." And the police should be finished with their investigation she thought.

"One o'clock?" he asked.

"Great. You have directions?"

"Pulled them off the internet for future reference. But I would like a phone number to reach you. One never knows what will come up."

"True, she murmured, rattling off her cell number. "See you later in the week."

By eight the next morning, Kyra walked along the beach, sipped a container of coffee and watched the sun, a golden glow rising out of the ocean and streaking the sky. She took a deep breath of the early morning air. The waves lapped between her bare toes splashing her ankles and cut—off jeans. The cold water sent icy tingles throughout her body.

Growing up on the Outer Banks in North Carolina, she used to jog along the shoreline with Brandy, her German Shepard who'd dive in and out of the surf. Her brothers would run with her, each competing against one another. None of them jogged for the fun of it, or to see the sun rise, or set, for that matter. They ran to win.

Odd, how one of the things the homicide Lieutenant mentioned was the beauty of each day's beginning and end. Someone who spent his working—life filled with death, noticed the breathtaking wonder of sea and sky.

"Kyra."

She turned as Tom's deep voice interrupted her thoughts and rumbled over the gentle swell of the waves. Her insides trembled as he sounded her name, or was it the sight of the powerful ease with which he moved. With cuffs rolled up, his kaki—clad long legs covered the beachfront in a couple of strides. He loosened his tie as he approached, undid the top buttons of his blue oxford shirt.

She recoiled at the sight of the armaments decorating his waist; gun, handcuffs, flashlight, pager, and cell phone. Though she herself walked around with a pager and a smart phone, she was chilled seeing his clipped alongside his gun.

We work in two different worlds, she thought. A murdered woman brought us together.

She dug her toes into the wet sand, waved, and called, "Good morning. How did you know where to find me?" Behind him she noticed his shoes parked up on the ridge. A navy blue blazer dangled from the half—opened gate leading to the cobbled stone pathway back to the house.

She burrowed into her Harbors Resort sweatshirt, rubbed the ball of one foot along her opposite ankle.

"You mentioned something to Rory before you left the Bed and Breakfast. Told her you were bringing some of your things over to the mansion."

"Couldn't sleep. I was up at five. So, I figured not to waste time I'll start moving over."

"I asked you to wait until we were through."

"I have work to do and appointments to confirm. I didn't think one day would make much of a difference to the police." She grew aware of his scent, lemony and fresh, as he caught up and walked alongside. "Do you play twenty questions with the B&B's owner, too?" she said unaccustomed to the sudden twinge of jealousy that tied her gut into a knot.

Embarrassment flooded her cheeks and she turned to face the sun. The inn's owner was tall and attractive, but she did wear a wedding ring. Kyra stole another glance at Tom's left hand. No ring, just a watch to tell the time. Time! If she had the time to be around for six months, or he had a position where he traveled extensively, but...

"She won't let me."

"What does that mean?" Confusion swelled inside, she couldn't believe that she cringed, afraid of the answer.

"Rory's my sister. Barney's wife." The steady sound of his breathing, as he tilted his head toward her filled her space.

She gave a sigh of relief.

He seemed to understand she found the answer pleasing. A small smile crinkled the corners of his mouth. His thick hair appeared dewy from showering, invoked images she shouldn't be having.

He rolled his sleeves to the elbows. His forearms, thick with muscle, threw her off center.

"Oh." She said and almost gleefully added how wonderful. But then a slow anger raged within unfurling to get out. Who the hell did Tom Braden think he was? Her keeper? And she snapped, "If I'm your only suspect and you're following me around, you have nothing, Lieutenant."

"That's a possibility. But I stopped off to chat with Rory, which I do in the mornings. Then I thought why not eat breakfast with Kyra and we can arrange a time schedule for the clean—up. Imagine my surprise when I found you were out and already here."

"Why? What's the big deal? I didn't intend to stroll through the murder room." Damn! Would that be the new name for the dining room? She imagined James—Enrico's face. Dinner is now being served in the main murder room.

"What I'm concerned about is that you might have been the intended victim. And if that is the case, the killer could try again?"

"Is there a serial killer on the Cape?"

"No. Why would you ask such a thing?" He stepped closer, his broad shoulders and powerful chest blocking the wild grass with the mansion high on the knoll.

She moved further back into the surf. "A serial killer doesn't need a motive." She stood on tiptoes, tilted her chin up. "And I can't imagine who has a motive to kill me."

She didn't have to remind herself, that this was her initial premise. It lay like a kernel of truth in the pit of her stomach.

"Got you. But me thinks, the lady protests too much."

She dropped her feet down flat in the sand. The water pooled above her ankles in the ridges her toes had dug. Her heartbeat dropped as well.

"The Whales Bay Chief of Police thinks you're more suspect than victim," Tom added in a somber voice.

"Meaning what?"

"We're checking alibis before we rule you out."

"Then you're not ready to arrest anyone, including me?"

"Correct."

"And what is your alibi? Being that you're so familiar or related to most of the people I've met since my plane landed." She forced herself not to focus on his face. Thank God, her eyes were hidden behind sunglasses, like his.

His laugh echoed along the beach. He pushed his glasses up, riveting his gaze on her face. She was taken back by the intensity of his expression, the sweet clarity in his eyes. A gasp caught in her throat. She had the wildest desire to kiss him, but instead concentrated on dragging her feet through the surf. She had to keep moving, stay focused on her agenda.

Sex wasn't listed. Sex was almost a figment of her imagination. Twenty—seven months since the last time.

She thought of the sex toy she had purchased and never used sitting in her night table drawer.

What a shame she wasn't the type to take a fling?

His voice resonated with remnants of his laughter. "I need you to come down to the station and sign a statement."

She needed to get on the computer and finish researching Biloxi, not hunger after a police lieutenant, not jump at his demands. Her life, her career might be at stake. She knew her priorities. Harbors Conglomerate had no plans scheduled for the Mississippi area. At least, none had existed before her flight to the Cape. So, why did the Chairman of the Board mention the country music resort city on the Mississippi river? Who knew what games James Enrico was playing? He could have set up this trip to the Cape as a ploy to get her out of the way. As a business legend, JE was a skilled master.

"I'll come by the police station this afternoon when I'm finished." She climbed up the flight of wooden stairs past the beach to the small foot shower near the rear gate of the house.

Tom yanked the faucet chain. Water poured from the spigot. "Let's push for this morning."

"I have to complete a report. Yikes." Tap Dancing from the cold flow, Kyra rinsed the sand off her feet, dried them in the grass, and slipped into sandals, waiting while Tom pulled on his socks and shoes.

"I'll drive you into town, as soon as I talk to my men." He swung his jacket over his shoulder.

"I'm not bolting anywhere. A couple of hours won't make a difference." She stepped ahead on the cobblestone path.

Tom heard Whales Bay Chief of Police Reed Williams bellow out his name. He looked towards the rear of the mansion. Williams stood in the doorway. The Chief sucked in his gut, using his height and thick shoulders to emphasize his authority.

Tom watched Williams' eyes narrow evaluating Kyra while frustration played hopscotch inside his mind. Technically, neither man reported to the other. But Tom understood why the Chief didn't want him around solving a high profile murder in the Whales Bay jurisdiction. If the state hadn't appointed Tom and his new division, the Chief would be in charge of this case.

Tom had worked well with other towns in the area. They all benefited. But Williams wanted what he wanted. And he didn't like Tom and his team usurping his domain. The chief was well known for his impeccable timing—turning up at the wrong moment. Like now!

"Who's that?" Kyra asked.

"Whales Bay Chief of Police Williams."

"The one who thinks I am a good suspect?"

"Don't know about good, but a suspect, yes." Tom's thoughts ticker—taped across his mind. He hoped she didn't acerbate the situation. "The Chief feels a JEC executive will earn him points in the media."

Ignoring his words, she picked up her pace extended her hand. "Kyra Stevens, Chief. Sorry to meet under such circumstances." She gave her pearly white smile.

Williams searched Kyra's face as if it held the answers to all the unsolved crimes on his books. "We preferred that you didn't move in until we finished going through the house."

"I'm living here for the next three months. It's such a big place; your men and I won't collide. The killer kept to one room."

Tom recoiled. Now, she went and did it.

Williams flushed purple. "How do you know that, Ms. Stevens? When did the perpetrator tell you that insightful piece of information?"

Without waiting for a response, he turned, snapping at Tom, "Did she sign a statement?"

"She! Do you mean me?" Kyra hissed.

"We have an afternoon appointment," Tom said in a sharp tone. "I'll fax over a copy of the report for your records."

"Does she have a lease we can look at? And whose name is the house listed in?"

Kyra fished out an initialed burgundy card case from her tote bag. Extracting an embossed gold letter business card, she handed it to Tom. "Lawrence Ellridge, the Boston attorney who handled the sale two years ago."

Seething, she stalked into the atrium—ceiling hallway. "I'll be upstairs working." Then pivoting about, her eyes flared. "Why in heaven's name would I need a lease? We own the place."

CHAPTER FOUR

Kyra printed out Ellridge's first monthly report then put in a productive hour on the computer comparing her figures and dates with his. She was almost finished when she spotted a glaring oversight between the two sets of numbers.

She reached for her phone, but stopped mid-air. Better to have a face—to—face discussion where she could see his reaction. Then she'd be able to judge if Ellridge made an honest mistake, or was he someone she had to watch.

The click of the bedroom door startled her. She whirled around as a wiry man hustled in muttering, "Ah, the redhead from Miami! Do you know the grief you caused?"

Kyra scrambled up from the desk flipping her laptop cover closed. "Who are you?"

"Detective Petersen." He flashed his badge, but before she could get a good look, he pocketed it and then proceeded to walk in a tight circle between her and the door.

"What do you want?" she demanded.

"To meet you." Petersen said breezily pulling the brim of a Boston Red Sox baseball cap over his forehead. A black mustache and beard covered the lower part of his face. But he couldn't hide his eyes, cold and narrow, they wandered in every direction.

"Why?" She took a half step. Her instincts screamed—get out. A killer was on the loose and it could be this stranger.

She inched another step hoping to circumvent the intruder. She didn't trust his squirrelly demeanor and prayed the Lieutenant hadn't left the building. Yet, if Tom was downstairs with the Crime Scene Unit, how did this bizarre man walk past, climb a flight of stairs and wind up in her bedroom?

"Why?" he repeated with a snarky grin. "Because you were a very lucky lady. And now, your luck has run out."

In an instant, Petersen pulled a large Maglite from his cargo pants. Taking a giant step forward, he swung the flashlight over his head and brought it down full force missing her by an inch.

Kyra jumped back gasping, reached behind her and grabbed JE's tennis racket off the top of her suitcase. Horrified, as once again, the man raised his Maglite, she screamed on top of her lungs and smashed the racket into his mid-section. Picking up her feet, she raced for the door.

A man's voice shouted, "Upstairs!"

The intruder grunted. Doubling over, he dropped his makeshift weapon. From the corner of her eye, she saw him grab the lamp off a night table and throw it at her.

Kyra ducked, felt a blow to her right temple, and heard the lamp crash to the floor. A flash of light blinded her and turned into intense pain. Her legs buckled and she sank to the corner of the bed.

She heard pounding on the stairs and Tom shouting, "Go to the left. I'll take the south wing."

"We'll meet again, Bitch. We're not finished," the man hissed. His words trailed after him as he ran into the hallway.

His threat rattled her insides. The soft hair on the back of her neck stood up. Something warm and wet trickled past her eye.

Kyra forced herself to stand by inching her hands along the quilt-ed coverlet and grabbing hold of one of the four-posters. Her legs gave way, but she pulled herself up by clutching the pole. Resting her cheek against the cool mahogany, she heard Tom's voice—far off—calling, "Kyra where are you?"

"In my bedroom, at the end of the hall," she screamed, but only a croak came out. She tried harder, this time a low moan escaped. She called out his name. Heard the crackling of her harsh whisper, just as Tom burst through the doorway.

"Kyra. Are you okay?" His shoes smashed on the lamp's broken glass. "What happened?" He reached for her upper arms pulled her towards him, holding her tight against his chest.

She leaned into him heard the beat of his heart, felt her eyes fill with tears of relief.

He made a small rubbing circle on her back. She let out a deep breath just as two uniformed policemen rushed in and without a word began searching the adjoining bathroom and alcove. At the sight the officers Tom let go and took a step back. Her legs felt wob-bly and she had to brace herself once again with one of the bed's four-posters.

"He tried to kill me."

"Who?"

"He said he was a detective."

"What?" The returning officers echoed Tom's response.

She recognized their skeptical tones. Her heart sank, different time, different reason. The man was a police lieutenant with a team that backed him up. She was the stranger in their midst.

She had to think, forced herself to focus.

"Maybe you should sit down." He took her arm walked her to a window chair.

"I'm okay," she said, shrugging him off. She had to stay on her toes. She felt off—center from the blow and was unreasonably upset that Tom didn't want his team to see he helped her stand.

"Get a Paramedic up here." He nodded to one of the cops who disappeared out the door. Then he handed her a tissue from the box on the desk.

She dabbed at the trickle of blood inching down her cheek. Reached for the bottle of water near the computer.

"Here! Let me." Tom removed its cap, placed the bottle in her hand.

Kyra swallowed several sips.

"Can you answer a few questions?"

She nodded her head.

"How old was he?"

"Hard to tell covered by all the fuzz."

"What fuzz?"

"Thick beard, a handlebar mustache."

"Color hair?"

"Black, but it wasn't real."

"What?"

"The beard and mustache; I'm positive they were fakes. Like something out of a Halloween disguise kit."

"Damn! What about his height?"

"Five feet eight—to—maybe ten inches."

"How did he get away?" Tom stepped to the windows facing the ocean. Pulling one open, he leaned out.

Kyra could see the waves, white capped and angry crashing against the beach. Sea breezes flowed through the apple green bedroom reminding her of home. She wanted to be there and not in this house of death and mayhem.

The older cop moved his hand to his gun.

Why?

Trepidation tugged at her insides. Did she alarm the officer? What did he expect her to do? Push the Lieutenant out the second floor window.

Tom yelled over his shoulder, "Several people on the beach. What was he wearing?"

"Cargo pants and a leather bomber jacket."

"What color jacket?"

"Black."

Tom cursed under his breath, took a second glance along the beach and spun on his heel. "The assailant is jogging toward the inlet. Take Danny and a Blue and White. Try to head him off. Tell the Crime Scene Unit to get up here and go over the place with a fine tooth comb."

He pulled the cell from his belt, repeated everything into the phone, and asked for backup ending with, "He could have a boat, or he's headed to one of the side roads where he left a car."

Tom stepped away as a Para—medic walked in, and began treating her wound. One guy and a woman wearing CSI jackets entered, nodded and unlocked their cases.

Tom sat on the desk straddling a corner. He refocused on Kyra. "What did he say?"

"That I was a real lucky lady whose luck had changed." She took a deep breath. "He flashed a badge. Said he was Detective Petersen." She winced from the antiseptic the Para-medic applied.

"There is no Detective Petersen on the Cape. Did you get a good look at the badge?"

"No." Kyra shook her head. "He backed me into a corner. I...I tried to get out. He had a Maglite. Swung and missed. I hit him with the tennis racket and ran for the door, but he dropped the search light, grabbed the lamp and threw it."

"He dropped the flashlight?" Tom repeated jumping up. He began combing the floor with the cops and crime scene investigators.

"Got it," One of them shouted, crawling from under the bed.

With gloved hands, Tom examined the flashlight before they bagged and labeled it.

He rested a hand on her shoulder, tilted her chin up to re-examine the dressed wound.

She shifted, stood, and braced a palm against his chest.

His eyes flashed concern, lingered on her face. He brushed the hair from her forehead.

This wasn't good. This reaction she had to him. The only result would be grief. She couldn't endure short—term flings. She needed the trappings and most of all—she needed time, always her constraint. She'd learned the hard way don't fall into bed, then leave and say good—bye, nice to have known you.

She needed a beginning, a relationship, and a closure. Her return was already set for late May, back to Miami, James Enrico, and her daily grind.

"Any ideas how he got into the house?" Tom continued.

"No." She stared blankly, had to stop her thoughts about him.

"We didn't pass or see anyone on the staircase. How many entrances are there?" He walked over to his men. "Did the Whales Bay Police secure all the doors after the murder?"

"They said they did." The lanky officer half turned, eyes glued to Tom's every move.

The older officer set his mouth in a thin line. "I heard small talk in Whales Bay's police station. There is a side door at the end of the hall, Sir. Looks like a closet. It leads to a back staircase that opens downstairs in the mudroom and goes out to the garden. Some of the men were questioning it. The intruder could have gotten in and out that way."

Kyra saw the pulse beating above Tom's jaw line. She realized he hadn't known, nor was told by the local police about this entrance.

From all her business meetings, Kyra had developed a sense of premonition and an instinct to analyze a situation. She too, found it hard to believe the town police hadn't discussed the garden entrance after they searched the house. Did they do a lousy job, or deliberately withheld information? Her stomach cramped. Either way, the new attempt on her life was the result.

Tom nodded to the Crime Scene Unit. "Let's see if our mysterious assailant left a trace. Go over every inch, down the stairs, in the mud room and out the garden." He rubbed his jaw. His voice boomed in the spacious silent room, "If you haven't already."

"By the time we arrived after the murder, Chief Williams said everything was under control. We were not involved in searching the house."

"Jeez!" Tom locked gazes with Kyra. "Lucky bast…" swallowed his words, paused, and added, "But we'll get him."

Kyra wondered, would they, and after how many incidents. A chill shuddered through her. The assailant had made it very clear she was high on his list—of—things to do.

And what about <u>her</u> list? Starting with Biloxi. Could she take the southern city out of the mix? It would be one less thing to worry about. First, she had to go on the computer and finish her search. Find out, if she could still abide by James Enrico's decisions. Or had she reached the beginning of the end? She was only one of a handful who survived and understood how the CEO operated.

"How long have you worked for JEC Industries?" Tom asked abruptly.

"Over seven years, my second job after graduating college." Where was the Lieutenant going with this line of questioning? She felt as if he was mirroring her thoughts.

⊷⊶

Tom glanced over at Kyra in the passenger seat. Behind the whooshing windshield wipers and torrential rain, the inside of the SUV seemed closed off from the rest of the world as they drove to the police station. His headlights sliced through the storm's midday darkness.

What was it about this woman that got under his skin? Even now sitting side by side, just feeling her breath in the confines of the vehicle, he felt connected. Ridiculous Braden, he told himself, she's playing you. Women like Kyra—beautiful and smart—competing in the national corporate world had groupies, powerful men vying for their attention. Which brought up James Enrico!

What did he mean to her? The business giant was an unknown entity over a thousand miles away, yet, permeated his murder case here on the Cape.

His case that was growing tentacles!

An intruder?

A primary witness—infuriatingly obstinate—who didn't stray from his thoughts?

The Whales Bay Chief of Police with a lapse in judgment?

Kyra could have been murdered. And Tom held himself responsible. It happened on his watch. He should have taken extra precautions. Yet, Williams wasn't known to be careless.

Tom turned north on Lower County Road that bisected the town. Sheets of rain pounded the car forcing him to accelerate the wipers. Kyra appeared lulled by there back and forth motion.

He thought too much, drove too fast. He tapped the brake. His gaze met hers in the mirror, and he wondered aloud, "Were you scheduled to meet with Andy McDermott?"

"Who?" She frowned.

"McDermott. He's the town's zoning commissioner."

"The name sounds familiar."

"He's Megan's husband. At work, she used her maiden name, Polk. Last summer, she took out a restraining order against him."

"It didn't do much good." A rasp sounded in her throat. "Oh God!" All of a sudden, she shot Tom a sideways glance of horror. "I saw black and blue marks on her thigh—I thought the murderer..." Her voice trailed off. "Were they old bruises made by her husband?"

"We don't know, yet." His voice tightened, an immediate reaction to her reluctance to answer questions until she was asked a second or third time. "When you stepped into the crime scene you saw much more than you originally said. Why hold back?"

Her face turned snow white, her tone sounded like an artic wind, "I'm sure bruising was in the ME's report. Why would you need my input? Tell me Lieutenant, why isn't McDermott the number one suspect on the Chief of Police's list, instead of me?"

"He knows Andy. You're an unknown entity." She had shot back her response—fast as a bullet. Not much got past her. "How familiar is McDermott's name?"

"I don't believe I ever met him, but I think my staff included him as a person of interest. Someone I should meet on my trip."

"And why is that?" He knew the answer while he asked the question.

"My company deals in real estate. If it's the same McDermott who's the Zoning Commissioner." Kyra flourished a hand. "Then it's just good business practice to touch base. One never knows where the next ball will land."

"This isn't a baseball game, Kyra. We're talking murder. You resemble the victim. You discovered her body in the house where you are staying. And now, you are planning several meetings with her abusive husband. Your life is intertwined with theirs."

She stared aghast. "I said McDermott might—might be a name on a list. And you're saying our lives are intertwined?"

"Too many coincidences."

The car filled with silence. The only sounds wind and rain and the wipers. She clasped her hands tight in her lap. "There are too many flaws in your logic Lieutenant".

"Such as?"

"I've never met these people nor have ever been in Massachusetts."

"Then why didn't you mention seeing black and blue marks on the victim, or how you got the victim's blood on your sneakers. You omitted telling me about entering the murder room and now, you mention plans of meeting with the dead woman's husband. We gather information to solve cases and prevent future incidents from happening."

"Is that how it works?" Her mouth tightened, her eyes narrowed.

"But most of all," he continued. "If the McDermotts are not the connection, then what is?"

"I don't know!" she snapped infuriated by Tom's calm controlled voice.

"Is there someone who wants to walk out of your life without splitting joint accounts, or joint assets?"

"I'm single."

"Engaged? Significant other looking for…"

"Lieutenant, I haven't had an affair in over two years. How about you?"

He gave a hollow laugh. His knuckles whitened as he gripped the wheel. "I'm a widower. Ivy, my wife died in an automobile accident several years ago."

Kyra gasped, reached out as if to grab his arm. "I'm so sorry," she whispered.

Tom forced himself to continue. "My son, Matt is seven. Rory is not only Matt's aunt; she's his baby sitter and friend. That's why I, sometimes we, stop in at the B&B to chat with her and plan his day-- not to follow you."

She stared at him, eyes wide, and cheeks colored red.

Kyra collected herself. What it must have taken for him to confide something so personal? She twisted around trying to look straight at him, but her shoulder belt pulled her back. "It had to be devastating—for you and your son." She hesitated. "I know you're trying to be kind, but I—I can't think of anyone who wants to kill me. I work ten to twelve hour days. Eat take out and curl up in front of the TV, if I don't have a report to complete. I'm really quite boring."

The dead woman in Miami and the redhead on the dining room floor—shouted otherwise. Kyra shivered inside her skin.

"What about the intruder in your bedroom?"

Her mouth went dry with terror. Would he ever stop with his insidious questions? Pick away at her life. Her eyes closed. Her head felt like a buzz saw was gnawing away.

"I can't ignore you, Kyra. Not so soon. You're our primary witness. Actually, our only one." A half smile touched the corners of his mouth. "McDermott isn't a peach of a guy, but..." Tom shrugged. "I'm bound by my position to keep an eye on you."

Her cell's chime jolted her. She reached for the phone dangling from her tote, saw the attorney's name, wished she could disconnect.

She pressed TALK.

"What is going on down there?" Lawrence's officious voice boomed in her ear. "Why didn't you tell me about the murder when we spoke last night?"

"What for? We'll talk at our meeting, tomorrow. I'm with someone, now. Bye." She hit END and let the mobile drop.

"Meeting with whom?" Tom asked.

"A business meeting."

"You have to do better than that." He shook his head and pulled in front of the police station. The concern in his eyes warmed her heart. Was it genuine?

He watched from the bow of his boat as the bedroom lights went out, drapes not fully drawn. The Bitch liked her ocean view. Tonight, she was sleeping in the mansion. He had no idea where she'd disappeared to the evening before.

He let his night vision goggles hang around his neck, poured the last drop of coffee and rum from his thermos. Draining its cup, he zipped his anorak up under his chin.

It was time to head back. Tomorrow would be a long day and he needed his wits about him to find the exact moment he could finish his job and notify the payer.

Would the garden door still be available to him, or did the police discover the entrance and seal it off?

Anyway, who was this scrappy lady from Florida? Rumor had it she was Cassal's girl friend, or JEC's next Chief Operating Officer. The e-mail said both were possibilities. That he had to be careful.

He started the motor. In the pounding surf, it didn't sound louder than the barest of whispers. He should have listened to his instincts. Should have gotten rid of Kyra Stevens before she boarded the plane for Cape Cod. Disregarded, what he was told. Don't kill her in Miami! Wait until she gets off the plane in Boston

Now what? He wouldn't allow anyone to pull his world down. No matter how many times he had to try. Murder always worked for him before.

CHAPTER FIVE

K yra sat alone at a table for two and once again checked her watch. Lawrence Ellridge was almost forty—five minutes late and still there was no sign of him. She had decided to meet the attorney at the small café on the mainland after learning the police would not be finished at the beach house for another day or two.

She felt a restaurant not frequented by Cape residents would be perfect. She didn't want to be seen dining with the real estate lawyer who was supposed to buy land options for the proposed Harbors Hotel. She never dreamed the man some colleagues called Mr. Precision couldn't find the place until he phoned thirty minutes ago.

Eyes riveted on the entrance, Kyra sat forward as a tall, thin man walked in, waved off the hostess after a few words and approached her table.

From his firmly set jaw down to his shoulders, rigid in a grey pinstripe, Kyra saw he was roaring mad. She had anticipated a difficult meeting, but hadn't expected him to arrive clutching his attaché as if he was about to attack someone with it.

Determined to stay on track, she gave a wide smile, stood and held out her hand as the man stopped. "Nice to finally meet you, Lawrence."

"We could've met someplace more convenient, if you were so willing to drive onto the mainland," he said in a sarcastic tone, giving the barest of handshakes.

"I'm sorry. But a real estate lawyer dining with a Harbors VP!" She grimaced.

"The point being?" he muttered, settling into the opposite chair and placing his attaché alongside his polished cordovan shoes.

"Real estate values could jump sky high and we'd never come in under budget." She found it difficult to believe he didn't realize something so obvious.

"What happened to our original plan? Take—out food at the mansion? Not discreet enough for you?"

"That was before the police arrived on Monday and still haven't left."

"Why?"

"Gathering evidence."

"Three days," he snapped. "And they're still going over the crime scene?"

He was counting.

So was she. "The case is high profile, Mr. Cassel's vacation estate and a murdered woman. But it has nothing to do with us, or our plans for a Cape Cod Harbors resort." Like a mantra, the words were replaying and replaying in her head.

"I read the newspapers." And in an icy tone, asked, "Any idea when they'll pack up and leave?"

"No. I'm not privy to the police's daily schedules." She swallowed a laugh thinking of her tentative cooking arrangements with the Lieutenant.

Taking a quick glance around the room, she noted, there weren't more than three occupied tables. "It's a good choice," she said with satisfaction. "I can't imagine many Cape residents will drop in on a stormy mid—week afternoon."

"I don't expect many people drop in at anytime."

Oh my, she thought, time to end the topic and move on to buying land and their dollar signs.

But he squelched any idea of a conversation by picking up his menu, studying it, and then flicking his finger at the waiter. He asked a dozen questions before placing his order.

Kyra rattled off her selection.

Lawrence leaned back as water was poured.

Kyra unfolded the napkin across her lap.

Lawrence took a slow sip, played with the stem of his glass. Hands large, nails manicured, he wore a chunky college ring, his expression benign. He stared across the table.

A year or so over fifty, Kyra thought, and a touch of silver streaked thinning sandy hair and salted his Van-dyke.

"Was a bank account set—up to cover the land purchases?"

"Of course." She stared back. He obviously didn't believe in small talk and she was now quite positive he hadn't made an oversight in his monthly report.

"How many signatures are needed on the checks?"

"The usual two—out—of—four." Kyra scrutinized him. Where was he going with this line of questioning? All she seemed to be doing—since arriving on the Cape—was answering questions. If they weren't the Lieutenant's, or JE's, now they were Mr. Ellridge's.

His expression changed as he eyed the plate of food the server placed before him.

Kyra took a bite of her grouper. "H'mm. Delicious! How's your steak?"

"Eatable," he grunted placing his fork and knife on the rim of the plate. "When I finished the last project for Mr. Cassel, you mentioned one—out—of—three signers would be sufficient for future deals."

Her senses tingled at the very thought. She couldn't stop the un-ease zipping up her spine. "That sounds like a misunderstanding," she said in a controlled tone.

"I would not misunderstand something so important."

"Neither would I. The executive board has a strict protocol for bank accounts. It's not something we negotiate. Two out—of—four signatures are required on all accounts. I'm afraid you will have to live with it. It is a JE doctrine."

By the time coffee was served, Lawrence had turned from irri-table to livid over her ten-page manual on buying land options and her questions concerning his first report. When she pointed out that the numbers he used did not agree with Harbors' figures, a shade of purple spread across his face.

"No major changes from your last job with Mr. Cassel," she quick-ly added. "Just a few updates. And we prefer you use Harbors' format instead of your own. Enter your figures, scan and forward. It simpli-fies everything."

Knuckles white, the lawyer slammed shut his attaché on the up-dated outline she prepared. Kyra envisioned him tossing the report in his circular file the moment he returned to his Boston office, or throwing it into a desk drawer where various copies from other proj-ects were probably stacked.

"Do you have any suggestions? Ideas?" she asked, goaded by his body language and silence. Better to nip whatever bothered him in the bud. Not let it fester. "If plausible, we can incorporate them."

"This isn't my first venture with Harbors, Kyra." His eyes were shuttered, dull as mud. "Don't worry. I do what I'm supposed to," he smirked. A humorless smile formed at the corners of his lips.

Mistrust settled over her shoulders like a wet blanket.

Kyra threw a fresh log into the living room fireplace. Stoked the embers with a poker hoping to take the damp chill out of the night air. Another roll of thunder swept through the house.

Her trip was not going according to plan. And nothing was going according to her business agenda. She still did not know what had upset Lawrence at lunch. He refused to say. She couldn't believe her choice of restaurants was to blame. And the subject of bank accounts and budgets hadn't come up until after they met. Lawrence had walked into the café itching for a fight.

Nor could she think of a factual reason why her gut insisted she find a back—up for his position. Besides to her astonishment, Ellridge did a one hundred degree turn concerning the murder. Quite different from yesterday afternoon when he'd lost his cool on the telephone. Today, the murder wasn't his main interest.

A sudden jolt hit her. Damn! Could he have spoken to someone about the killing?

But who? The Chief of Police! This could account for the change in his demeanor. Especially, if Ellridge learned she was a murder suspect and he believed—hoped—she wouldn't be around much longer. Perhaps arrested! Kyra cringed at the thought. Maybe he was covering all his bases to make sure he had access to all the funds he needed if she was out of the way.

Lightening cracked the sky and lit up the ocean. She shot a glance at the wall of windows. The second day and the storm showed no signs of dissipating. Early March was not exactly the idyllic beach season James Enrico predicted, in more ways than one.

By now, JE's favorite vacation get—away was giving her a blazing headache. She rubbed the side of her forehead, closed her eyes for the briefest of moments and headed towards the kitchen. Putting some takeout in the microwave, she tapped in the cook time and waited staring aimlessly out the window. A pair of eyes stared back at her through the half-tilted kitchen blinds. She screamed and froze in place. A figure jumped back and took off toward the garden. His head covered by a hoodie.

The lights went out.

Kyra pushed herself to move and grabbed the wall phone, but the line was dead. After carrying her Smartphone since she left Florida, now she couldn't remember where she put it.

The room was pitch black. Feeling her way to what she hoped was the right closet, she gathered up several candles. The kitchen flashlight hung near the swinging door and she put the long lanyard around her neck.

The front bell clamored through the house like an echoing clap of thunder. Kyra jumped. Her pulse raced into overdrive. Who was out there?

She made her way into the living room, grabbed a poker, circled back past the dining room, and hurried to the front door. "Who is it?" she called holding her breath. Did a murderer announce himself? Was it the guy in the hoodie?

"Lieutenant Braden." Tom's deep voice came through the door.

Her heart leaped into her mouth. She felt like she conjured him up. She hadn't seen him since yesterday when she left the police station and Officer Pirro drove her home.

Suddenly, she felt like a boomerang hit her. What if Ellridge had connected with the homicide Lieutenant? Phoned him? Perhaps, the lawyer did a—round—about. Stopped off before today's luncheon—to get the dirt on her. Could she have been compromised?

The Lieutenant was seeking information for his own reasons. Ellridge had his. There was a great deal of money available to bank the resort. Everyone wanting his or her share. There were cities and counties where bribes were part of the local transactions.

Kyra tapped in the security code, cracked open the door. "What's the matter?" she demanded.

Tom stood dripping wet under the portico. "The power is down this side of the road. Are you all right?"

"Yes, but someone just ran behind my house. Was it one of your men?"

"No. I'm alone. Let me take a look. Close the door," his words blew away as he headed toward the side of the building.

Why had he taken the time to check on her? It had been years since someone showed such consideration. At Harbors, the assumption was Kyra Stevens took care of herself.

Before she could catch her breath, he was back pounding on the front door. "Kyra, open up. No one there," he panted as she fought with the door. The wind howled driving sheets of water straight at him and through the partial opening where she stood. She tasted the rain as it struck her face.

Water sloshed down her shirt pasting it to her chest. Wet jeans clung to her thighs. "You better come in." She managed to swing the door wide and stepped back into the hallway pushing damp strands of hair behind her ear.

A five o'clock shadow darkened his cheeks giving him a brooding look. Edgy! Dangerous!

Water dripped from his slicker to his boots forming a puddle at his feet. She felt like a fool. Where was her Southern hospitality? This wouldn't be happening in her parent's home. "Please, take off your slicker. You're soaked."

Tom shut the door behind him.

The lights dimmed on, then off.

"Do you have candles, other flashlights?" he asked.

"I scattered them around the house. Can I get you a towel?"

"Won't be necessary." He hung his bright yellow oilskin on the coat rack in the entrance hall, his gaze drifted to the poker still held in her hand. His expression told it all. She'd prepared for a murderer who rings the bell.

She cringed inside, gave a half smile. "I restarted the fire. It'll be warmer." She led him towards the living room past the crime scene tape flashing the light before her spilling shadows all around them. Kyra felt a surge of uneasiness. It had been a long day. She was tired.

Dealing with Lawrence.

Worrying about the police.

Handling James Enrico.

Thinking about Tom.

Definitely not thinking about playing one of his trivia games. Thinking about him looking broad and handsome and in control.

The lights went on, then off.

"Are all the doors locked?" His voice sounded hoarse. He flicked his flashlight back and forth.

"I checked them earlier. Set the alarm. But I..."

"Turned it off," he finished. "To let me in."

She stopped short at the living room threshold. He almost bumped into her; standing so close she felt his breath against her hair. He splayed one hand across the back of her waist. A big guy, he made her feel protected. Besides he was hot and she was attracted to him, a heady combination. She didn't need hormones speaking for her. They might say what she really wanted. An intimate relationship she didn't have time to build.

"What's the code?" he asked.

She sucked in her breath. Her muscles tensed, and then tightened into knots.

His hand dropped from her waist. "You want to reset it yourself?"

"Yes." She knew he'd felt her reaction, but she had nothing to apologize for. She had no idea—what it would take—for her to trust him, but at this very moment, she had no intention of giving Tom her security code.

She turned retracing her steps to the front of the house. He grabbed her hand, curling a finger around her thumb. But it was so dark and the beam of light so narrow, she had to wonder. Was he being thoughtful, or making a move on her? She hoped he couldn't hear her heart thumping.

He let go, stepped back and turned his head.

She punched in the security code. Her heart pounded in a staccato beat. He seemed a decent enough guy, but he had the power to set roadblocks in her path. And she wasn't privy to his exact relationship with Chief Williams. She needed to be careful. Right now, she had enough problems to grapple with and sex wasn't one of them.

For an instant, standing in the darkened hallway, Tom forgot all about the murder and the reason why he was in the mansion. All he could think of was the sensual woman with the wet blouse pasted to her chest. He needed to stop the heat coursing up his body. He had to concentrate on the how, who and why of his case. "Can we talk for a few minutes? I've a few questions."

"Don't you always." She stalked off.

He followed down the hall like an over—sexed teen-ager. The view from behind was as great as the view from the front. Her smooth easy stride stirred a hungry desire. You've got it bad, Braden.

He forced an official expression on his face.

The fire threw shadows across the room. Tom stood in front of the flames warming his hands. He had been one of New York City's finest; and now headed Massachusetts Homicide Division on the Cape, but this smart, sexy lady didn't trust him.

Was she afraid, if she gave him the security code, he'd break in? Perhaps sell it on E-Bay? Frustration welled inside. How could he reach her? Logically would be good.

"Is the Crime Scene Unit finished?" Her voice sounded distracted. She sank into the corner of the sofa.

"For now. They had one or two questions. Said you disappeared." Reviewing her signed statement raised his own questions. Better to put them on the back burner.

"I had a business meeting."

51

"Have you thought about what I asked?" He sat down, turned to face her.

"You asked so many things?"

"Who's after you?"

"You don't give up." She gave him a belligerent look.

"What do you think happened?"

"Megan was the victim. I'm just the red headed woman who found the body." She lifted her chin in challenge.

"I don't believe it." He focused on her face. "And neither do you. You said there was no one recent. How about someone out of your past?"

"You have a vivid imagination."

But a flicker passed across her eyes—what? Fear? Remembrance? "Someone who hasn't been in the picture for a while," he continued.

"Gregg," The name shot out of her mouth.

Tom didn't know who was more startled, Kyra or him? "Who is Gregg?"

"Gregg Henry Preston. We dated five—six weeks." She swallowed a deep breath.

"When?"

"Almost two—and—a—half years ago."

"And?"

"It ended. Just…" Her eyes stared into the fire—seeing another place, a different time. She pivoted her body towards Tom. "He kept popping up," she cried rigid with fury.

"Popping up?"

"At a club. My favorite café. The beach. I never felt so vulnerable. I was even afraid to go into the water."

"And?"

"I stopped running into him. It couldn't have anything to do with Cape Cod."

"Then why is it still on your mind?"

"His new girlfriend said I stalked him."

"Did you?"

"Give me a break. Do you think I'm capable of that?" Her words hung between them.

"No, I don't." Tom met her gaze. Held it.

She gave a sigh of relief.

"Why did his girlfriend say that?"

"I guess I'd show up. And there they were. Or after I'd arrive, they'd come in."

"You frequented the same places when you were together. Right?"

"Mostly."

"You knew the places. He knew them."

She nodded. Her face brightened like a little girl with her favorite ice cream flavor.

He hated to rain on her parade. "When did it start again?"

Her eyes opened wide like a frightened doe. She gasped, "How do you know?"

It took all his control not to put his arms around her. Hold her safe. She looked so vulnerable.

"It doesn't matter how, just tell me when." That's it, Braden, play big, strong policeman. He could've kicked himself.

"Last summer," she snapped. "Whose side are you on?"

"I'm looking for information, to help you. Don't clam up on me, Kyra."

"This happened more than sixteen hundred miles away. I don't think Gregg's ever been on Cape Cod, or in New England, for that matter."

"That's what hit men are hired for." He shot her a dangerous look. "You said no one was out to get you. Now, you mention a Gregg, who stalked you. Tell me about him. And then about last summer."

He moved closer. Reached over and touched her hand. At least, she didn't pull away. Her palm turned outward. He touched her thumb. Then interlaced his fingers with hers.

"I'd catch glimpses..." Her voice trailed off.

53

"How long did this go on?"

"Two—three months into September."

"Did you report it to the police?"

"Why? What was there to report? He made it sound I was lucky he didn't report me. But I knew. He knew. It was Gregg. He was stalking me. He said vice—a—versa." Her eyes flashed as if she was defying Tom to say it wasn't so.

"Everyday?"

"No. Mostly on weekends. He works—lives in Fort Lauderdale. You have to understand. He knew my shopping routine. I'd arrive. He'd be in the dairy section, or he'd come in a few minutes after me. But no one has so many coincidences."

"He threw your excuse back at you. Said it applied both ways."

"Yes."

"Did you change a restaurant, or supermarket?"

"Yes. But within a week or two, he'd show up at the new one." Perplexity creased her forehead. "And then, of course, there was the phone."

"What about it?"

"It would ring. When I'd answer, the caller hung up."

"When was this?"

"Started just after we met."

"How long did it last?"

"Months. Until we stopped running into each other."

"Simultaneously?"

"Yes. Once I stopped running into him, seeing him around. The calls discontinued."

"What about last summer?"

"The hang-ups started again. A couple of days before I recognized him in my rear view mirror on my way home from work."

"Which phone number did the calls come in on?"

She glanced at him in surprise. "Only on my home phone," she whispered. "Why did you ask?"

"You have several phone numbers, correct?"

"Yes. And in July, I flew home for my brother, Charlie's wedding. As far as I know, there were no calls in North Carolina, or on my cell. When I returned to Florida, they had already tapered off like they did a couple of years ago."

"When he stopped following you?"

"Yes."

"What about the office?"

"Not any calls that I know of."

"Do you have a picture of Gregg?"

"No."

He saw the expression on her face. "Did you burn them, or cut them up?" he teased.

"Both!" She glared at him.

"They would've helped to identify him."

"Why? You're going to Florida to look for him?"

"What does he do for a living?"

"He's a curator at the South Florida Museum."

"Miami and Fort Lauderdale are over an hour apart."

"Yes. He has a condo about forty-five minutes from me. When I met him," she gave a soft chuckle, "He appeared so self possessed, quiet." Her voice cracked. "Guess I made a bad judgment call."

He engulfed her hand in his. "Kyra, are you positive you didn't tell anyone?"

"When I was in North Carolina I almost told two of my brothers, Charlie and Josh. They're both with the FBI. But...Charlie was getting married and Josh was best man and what good would it have done? Gregg's in Florida and he isn't someone to take lightly."

"Quite scary," Tom muttered. Mr. Preston had intimidated her. Tom was surprised. He wouldn't have thought anyone could intimidate Kyra Stevens. It made him wonder what else she was holding back.

"Would you like a hot drink? Coffee, tea?" She hugged herself as they stood, felt her limbs shivering.

"No thanks. Don't want to overstay my welcome."

She gave a half smile, but her eyes were haunted.

He looked down the darkened hallway. "Maybe I shouldn't leave."

The phone rang and Kyra jumped. "They must have turned it back on."

"Take it easy," he called after her.

She disappeared into the curve of the alcove. Quickly, he walked after her, stopped and lingered as she answered, then heard her gasp. Slowly, she dropped her hand, the receiver dangled. A dial tone echoed in the stillness.

He hurried toward her, put out his arm encircling her, pressing her sideways against him thigh—to—thigh. Her hair smelled like spring flowers. He thought his heart would burst. "What?" A hang-up, Tom thought she would say.

"He said I was next."

"Who?"

"The man who attacked me in my bedroom," her tone escalated with each word.

She stared up into his eyes, a look of sheer panic on her face.

He felt the familiar tightness above his groin that struck him whenever she was near, and he brushed her lips with his.

CHAPTER SIX

Tom cradled her head with one hand ran his fingers through her long curly hair with the other. "Kyra." Murmuring, he kissed her eyes and cheeks and then slowly her neck.

She clung to him, arms wrapped around his waist, knees shaking. She couldn't leave go.

His lips were burning, yet tender. The rough stubble of his beard ignited her senses. When his tongue parted her lips and slipped into her mouth, she moaned with a heated delight.

Her head spun. Her knees buckled. She swallowed his breath, felt the wetness between her legs. He pressed her body into his. She felt his arousal rigid against her belly her nipples grind into the hardness of his chest and heard their hearts beating as one.

At the very moment she thought she would faint, he slowly released her. Ran his hands down her arms and stepped back with a sharp indrawn breath.

Kyra swallowed hard, belly fluttering; she couldn't focus on what Tom was saying. Only heard, "Now's not the time."

What's not the time, for their passion, their feelings? She leaned against the wall. A feeling of sadness filtered through her.

Tom picked up the phone she had dropped and pressed several buttons. Holding the receiver tight to his ear, he spoke low, reached out and touched the back of her hand.

She couldn't move.

He hung up. Punched in a different set of numbers. "The caller phoned from a throw away cell." He spoke in a staccato beat. His voice struck every nerve in her body. Saying goodbye, he disconnected and dialed for a third time.

He took a step or two closer, tried reaching out and brushed the back of her hand. Used his fingers to wrap around her thumb.

She yanked her hand away walked out of the alcove and sank into a chair.

Tom's authoritative tone flowed into the hallway. She blocked his words out. Didn't want to know whom he was talking too, or why. She heard him make another call.

Then he must have hung up for suddenly the phone rang.

She jumped. Who would he be calling? Was there another threat on her life?

"It's for me," Tom shouted before he answered. The man was so positive, so very sure about everything even knew what she was thinking.

"I'm going to stay overnight. I've made arrangements for Matt. Who knows what the assailant will do next?" he said walking toward her.

Kyra's eyebrows rose, chest heaving, hands grasping the arms of the chair, she waited, couldn't answer. He wanted her, not just wanted to keep her safe, but was there a difference?

She knew there wasn't a chance their relationship would work. They were bound by too many responsibilities.

His job.

The case.

He had too little time.

She had even less.

"Rory is keeping Matt overnight." He had taken care of his first responsibility, the most important one.

But she didn't want to be treated as the second. "I'm too old for a baby sitter, Lieutenant. You can go home."

She felt washed out and drained. Just a few minutes earlier, her need had made her forget why she traveled up the coast, why she was here and who she was. Her need had been this man. But he went and shut everything off like he closed a spigot.

"I don't want to leave you alone in this mausoleum," he added.

She laughed out loud. "Wait till James Enrico hears this one. A three million dollar mausoleum! The doors are locked and I can re-set the alarm. I'll be fine." She brushed past moved to the coat rack and held his slicker out. Tom grasped it as it slid from her fingers.

"Kyra, I had to learn where the call was made from. And I wanted to hold you all night not here in a doorway."

"It was just a moment. Sometimes it happens between a man and a woman. A quick kiss and one or the other walk away before they both get hurt."

His face froze as if he was punched hard in the gut.

She pulled the door open, said goodnight, and pushed it shut behind him.

He disappeared into the rain and wind.

Her instincts said let him go. Her body wanted him to return.

Automatically, she locked up, flashed her light toward the stairs. They seemed to disappear into a black abyss. Shining the light a few feet ahead, she made her way up to the bedroom.

"Tomorrow," she said aloud, wanting to hear a voice in the cold darkness, even if the voice was hers, "Tomorrow will be better. The electricity will go on, the monsoon will stop, the sun will come out and everything will go according to plan."

Kyra crossed her fingers.

She felt the early morning sun as it filtered through the vertical blinds. For the first few minutes she dared not open her eyes in case she was dreaming that sunny rays were caressing her face. She wondered would Tom still be beside her in the king—sized bed, if he had stayed?

During the night, she awoke, the house ablaze with lights, her body aching just thinking about him. Everything blinking and beeping, the electricity turned back on.

Now, she counted the days since they met.

Four! That wasn't many.

But that's how it started with Gregg. Except without the strong sexual tension. The raw chemistry between her and Tom couldn't be denied. She didn't remember feeling so intoxicated with any other man she had dated. But she had to face who they really were, officer—in—charge—of and prime witness—in—a murder investigation. By evenings end, he had made her feel like he was supervising a cat and mouse tournament. And she was the main player in the tournament. She refused to let him talk her into anything. She needed to keep his warnings at bay.

The phone threat was real, the voice sounded exactly like the intruder in her bedroom.

Goose bumps went up and down her arms and the same old question resurfaced. Who in heaven's name would want to kill a Harbors Acquisitions Vice-President?

Surprisingly, lying in the bed a little while ago, half awake, a dozen people popped into her head. Not good. Not good at all!

Her gut reaction said she needed Tom Braden as a friend. It was her best bet for an alliance, but becoming involved emotionally would not work. His sexuality was an anagram for trouble.

Her course of action was simple enough. Maintain a working relationship similar to the ones she had with other men in her professional life.

Though it was bad timing after last night, she did need one of the information—exchange dinners—Tom had accepted tongue—in—cheek. Perhaps this evening. Why not? She would see how this first one went and what information she could glean from it.

James Enrico was pressing for data. She would feed Tom food and afterwards feed James Enrico what she learned.

A good way to show the Lieutenant that one little kiss was not her panache. She could act as cool as he did. And JE would be content believing he was on top of things. Deep down she knew for one reason or another, she didn't have a choice. It was the best she could do in maintaining her status.

She ignored the little voice that murmured, "Just another excuse to see him tonight."

Kyra bounded out of bed, flew from bedroom to bathroom and back. Her day was beginning. She set up her itinerary, swallowed a cup of coffee and with a flair of anticipation drove into town.

The lemon-yellow sun lit up the world, the sky a brilliant shade of azure blue. Green sprouted everywhere; trees, lawns, the small, circular park in the center of town. Green like Tom's eyes. The thought of them threw a ray of white-hot heat through her body.

The Whales Bay Office of Records was in Town Hall, a red brick and white shingled building that also housed the Police Station where Tom had driven her two days prior. Though his regular office was in Hyannis Port, he had set up a temporary base in Whales Bay and shuttled back and forth. She wondered if he was in the building.

Kyra pulled into a visitor's spot and pushed through the front door following the signs along the glass and polished interior.

As she entered the records office, a tall, blond young woman with a long, mass of curls and granny eyeglasses walked towards her. The desk sign said Lilly.

Later, after two hours of pouring through tax records and property deeds, Kyra said to the young woman, "I'm renaming you, <u>A Wealth of Information.</u>"

Lilly laughed, her cheeks turning a bright pink. "Do you have everything you need?"

"I think so. Thanks a lot." Putting her laptop in her attaché, Kyra strode to the doorway, and turning said, "I owe you lunch." She backed out waving, and bumped into a uniform coming down the hall.

"Ms. Stevens, what are you doing here?" Chief of Police Williams blocked her path. "Lost?"

Kyra whirled around. "Research on property taxes."

His eyebrows went up a notch. "Why?"

"My boss asked me too."

"Harbors is thinking of building on the Cape?"

"More likely—thinking of selling. The murder in Mr. Cassel's dining room has put him in a fowl mood. The man is fastidious. So much blood where he entertains has upset him."

The Chief snorted. "I'd like to meet Mr. Cassel. Get his fix on the murder."

Kyra choked. James Enrico would have a heart attack. Deadpanned, she looked up at Williams. "That's why he employs lawyers. And me. We run interference."

"You don't count. You're a suspect." Chief Williams winked. "Can I help you find your way out?" He attempted to place his hand on her elbow.

"It's not necessary. You've done a great job color coding the halls and doors." She sidestepped briskly taking off for the exit. "Have a good day, Chief."

"As long as strangers don't kill anyone, Ms. Stevens, my day will stay good."

Kyra halted for the briefest of moments, stunned at the words spewing out of his mouth.

"And what about local residents? They never murder anyone? Or that doesn't bother you?" Her annoyance flooded her senses. She picked up her stride felt his eyes bore into her back and then the whoosh of a door. She gave a quick glance down the corridor as she hustled around the corner. Williams had entered the records office.

Kyra pressed the automatic opener for the front entrance and breathed in the fresh air.

She was positive Lilly had put everything back where it belonged. The large binders overflowing with computerized records and the blank computer screen left no clues. Chief Williams would only receive general answers to his questions. Lilly was busy with her own paper work and hadn't paid much attention to what Kyra was researching. She wouldn't have an inkling of the details Kyra noted in her laptop.

⇥ ⇤

Kyra was running late. She expected Tom any minute. She'd wanted to be out of the kitchen and pouring cocktails when he arrived.

She made a mental list of what she wanted to discuss with the Lieutenant so she could appease JE.

Turning the oven low to keep the lobster casserole warm, she started the salad. The front bell echoed through the house. Kyra quick stepped down the hall.

Tom filled up her doorway. In his hand a bouquet of flowers, a rainbow of tea roses. The man was full of surprises.

Her cheeks smarted. "Thank you, but you didn't have to."

"Na, dinner could be superb and you might ask for state secrets." He gave that Braden smile. "Then where would I be with just tidbits of information?"

Her gut twisted. Cat and mouse. But he did take her breath away. A stray curl fell across his brow. His eyes reflected the dark skies behind him holding unknown secrets. A burgundy silk shirt clung to his massive shoulders and narrow waist. And the jeans?

His jeans so smooth and sleek over his long legs left very little to her imagination. A shiver of desire raced through her body. Come on, girl? Get a grip. Stick to the itinerary.

"Smells great," he said following her to the kitchen and glancing into the dining room as they passed.

The man was always on the job checking things out.

"Lobster casserole." She found a vase, filled it with water, arranged the flowers and set them on the table in the curve of the kitchen bay window. "Pretty. Thanks, Tom. They look great." She smiled. "I'd thought we'd eat in here. They're first taking the carpet away tomorrow and the painters don't start until Monday."

She went back to the salad. Thin slices of cucumber on a bed of greens decorated with shredded carrot and curls of radish.

"Typical after—work dinner?" Tom inched a radish from under her knife.

"Be careful, Mr. Detective." She raised the knife an inch or two above the cutting board then cringed. God, what must he think?

But he seemed to take no notice.

"I do it to relax—a couple of nights per week. Have a few friends in." She diced up a tomato and large plump olives.

Tom sneaked an olive away.

Kyra playfully hit his hand.

"Heard you raised Chief Williams' blood pressure today." Tom leaned over the granite island a twinkle escaped from his emerald eyes and crinkled at the corners.

Her heart did a tumble Sault. She wasn't sure why? Was it the man? Was it the spy network? Didn't matter. She shook her head. "What a town?" Handed Tom the salad bowl, and motioned to the table. "The CIA could use this place for a training ground." She propped herself, one hand on the counter—top, and one hand on her hip.

Tom placed the bowl next to the vase of flowers. "What's the point in antagonizing Williams? It can only hurt you."

"I don't like to be accused of cold—bloodied murder." Her voice harsh, she tried softening her tone, but wound up gritting her teeth.

"He accused you? Today, in the hallway?"

"Jeez! You even knew where we were standing." Disbelief rocked her. Astounded, she followed him with her eyes. "He called me a suspect."

"That's not..."

"It's the same thing." She threw the salad scrapings in the garbage, rinsed her hands and brushed past to open the frig. She took out the chilled strawberry daiquiris and the spinach dip with crackers. They moved to the fireplace in the living room.

"Now, I am impressed." Tom said after a sip. "Cheers. Here's to a wonderful vacation."

They clicked glasses.

He smiled. "And a great business trip."

"I wish you would have called me," she said.

"When?"

"When you and Williams were discussing why I was in the records office."

"Which reminds me, why were you there?"

A grin played around the corners of his mouth.

"Researching property taxes. By the way, that's the same answer I told Chief Williams."

"Oh! I hoped you were in the building to see me." Tom looked crest fallen. "So you weren't covering with Williams."

Kyra sat there like something hit her in the gut. She blinked, knew her face registered absolute surprise. "I better check on dinner," she mumbled scrambling to get out of the room. Was he serious, or was he playing her?

She turned off the oven, reached for the oven mitts. Decided to dim the lights.

Felt him behind her before she even heard his step. She couldn't speak.

"How are we doing?" he asked in a throaty voice.

"Dinner is served," she managed to announce. Well, no one could say she hadn't killed romance for this evening. Wasn't that the way she wanted it?

Tom poured the wine. The lady had a temper. And a body. And a...
He got himself back to reality.

"Here's to a pleasant evening. Thanks." He tilted his head toward
her, took a slow sip.

Her cheeks burnished copper against the white porcelain of her
skin. Tendrils escaped from her French braid and she held the wine
glass too tight.

"I've been thinking about what you said before. You're right, you
know. But I've learned to live with Williams."

"I don't have too. Is he your boss?"

"No." We work separately, but have to coordinate. He runs the
Whales Bay Town's Police Department. I'm with the State. Higher up
on the totem pole. The problem is he feels threatened by me." His
eyes locked with hers.

In a stern voice, Kyra spoke dryly, "I've worked very hard to get
where I am. And all he's doing is dragging my name through the
mud."

"Then the faster we solve this crime the better for all of us."

Kyra tilted her head. "True. But yours will be instant gratifica-
tion. You'll have to cross swords with him over another case, sooner
or later." Her heart melted and she felt sorry. She knew the cold,
tight cramp of anger that existed in many workplaces.

She nodded towards Tom's dish. "Do you like?"

"Yes. Very much." His eyes drifted to her face with deliberation
and lingered.

CHAPTER SEVEN

The breeze picked up Tuesday morning as Tom left the Whales Bay Police Department. Turning his jacket collar up, he pulled the keys from his pocket.

Over a week since Megan McDermott's murder and he hadn't made any headway in today's briefing with the Chief of Police. Williams had left for the town council meeting leaving Tom to review the Whales Bay McDermott file.

This had frustrated him even more. There were too many gaps, too little information, page numbers missing and nothing new to add to his bureau's reports. Tom had hoped it would be just the opposite, Whales Bay's murder book and files overflowing. Yet, the data accumulated by his men doubled that of the Chief's investigators.

Whales Bay was where the crime had taken place. Where Williams and his squad knew the people who lived and worked in the area. Perhaps that was the underlying cause of the problem. The Chief did not want to question or antagonize loyal constituents.

It was this attitude within some of the smaller towns that made the Governor set up Tom's bureau and team. The Governor also felt it was time to centralize tech support throughout the State.

Tom knew Williams abhorred the entire idea. And was trying to delay the conversion of all his department's records. "Enough info was on computers. They didn't need any more to be added." His remarks were well known along the eastern seaboard. "Let's get back to basics."

Today, the only good thing that came out of their meeting was that the Chief agreed to have a patrol car do drive-bys around the Cassel estate. Tom also coordinated with his team and arranged for a car to pick-up the slack.

Now, unlocking his car, he tossed his attaché on the passenger seat, and heard Barney shouting, "Tom, Tommy."

Turning around, he saw his brother-in-law rushing along the square's diagonal path from the direction of Town Hall.

"Wait up," Barney yelled. His ponytail and tie were blowing every which way in the gusty wind. With hands shoved into in his tweed blazer pockets, he headed across the road ignoring the oncoming traffic.

Amazingly, all the cars braked and stopped short; only one sounded a horn. Tom shook his head, grinning. "I thought there was a law against jay—walking."

"Nah. Anyway, no one wants to be charged with running down the Mayor."

"What's happening?"

"I was hoping to catch you. Do you have time for lunch?"

"Sure?"

Bucking the wind, they headed up the block to the Crossroads Diner.

"Can't believe spring is around the corner." Barney gave a slight shiver as he took the front steps two at a time.

"Rough meeting?" Tom asked picking up on his brother—in—law's mood.

"Andy McDermott," Barney muttered between tight teeth. He nodded to half—a—dozen patrons and slipped into the end booth. "Disrupted the entire meeting."

"Even I have to admit, the man is in a difficult position. People focus on him as the victim's husband, or the primary suspect—if not both." Tom stopped talking as the waitress approached. Smiling, he declined the menu, and ordered, "Two eggs over with bacon, rye toast and coffee."

"The same." Barney grimaced. "Rory insists breakfast is the most important meal of the day. But some mornings there just isn't time, so I brunch." He jutted his chin towards Tom. "Your excuse?"

"Ditto! I try to eat with Matt whenever I can, but sometimes..." He shrugged. "It's damn hard. Rory's indoctrinated. She can't help it. Swears by our mother's ten rules for a healthy life. Breakfast is number four."

"What's number one?"

"Ask her." Tom winked, hesitated and regarded Barney with a level expression. "Is Andy complaining the police aren't doing enough to find his wife's killer?"

"You got it."

"And the Police Chief is...?"

"On his side," Barney cut him off. "Heard it so many times, I know the entire scenario by heart. But, and this is a new one, the State Police, Lieutenant Braden in particular, is harassing him."

"He beat her, Barney. Her body was covered with bruises."

"Claims the murderer did that."

"The bruises were old."

"They've been separated for months."

"They got back together. Were living in the same house for the past month."

"The house belonged to his family. Once she returned, he couldn't get her out. The place is loaded with antiques. Andy was afraid to leave her there alone. That she would ransack the place."

The waitress set their food down. Both men waited for her to walk away.

"They had a pre-nup." Tom sprinkled pepper on his eggs. "She would have had to return anything she took."

"Pre-nups mean nothing to a good lawyer." Barney smiled and waved to the far side of the diner.

"She took out a restraining order against him."

"And then rescinded it."

"The Whales Bay police didn't enforce it. So she said what the hell. Why should she bother?"

"How do you know?"

"Her parents. They had already cut short their trip, and were about to return north when she was murdered. The night before the murder, Megan told them Andy was having an affair."

"With whom?"

"Megan never told them the name. But her mother said it was someone local. It could be the reason behind the murder."

Barney glanced away, sat back and ran a finger around the rim of his coffee cup. "The McDermott family holds a lot of weight in this town."

"Oh. So we should let Andy get away with murder? Wife—beating wasn't enough? Megan called the police several times. They did nothing." Tom leaned forward, searching his brother—in—law's face.

"No." Barney stared back. "But the town needs the case solved quickly. The primaries are in six months. Andy is a damn good zoning commissioner. Knows his stuff. Would hate for him to lose to a hack. And a hack is getting ready to run against him. Plus, the tourist season is almost upon us. Unsolved murders leave a bad taste in everyone's mouth. The board is afraid we'll lose seasonal renters and dailies."

He tore the corners on two sugar packets poured the contents into his coffee, and stirred. "Andy shouldn't bear the brunt of all the gossip. We shouldn't throw him to the wolves, unless we're one hundred per cent positive he's guilty. Someone has to protect him."

"Protect him!" Tom repeated.

"Yes. Not try him in the media. He could be innocent. Andy suffered enough. Kyra is beautiful and charming, but she's a stranger."

"That makes her what—automatically guilty? I can't believe you're saying this."

"I played with Andy in the schoolyard. We went to day camp together."

"I heard he was a bully—even back then."

"Stuck up for his rights and his friends. That's not a bully; and it's a long way from killing someone. I can't see him cutting his wife's throat. Neither can the Chief of Police."

"But you don't find it difficult believing a beautiful, intelligent executive without a motive could overpower a woman the same size, slit her throat and have no marks or blood on her body or clothes?"

"That sounds more like a Personal Ad for a date than a…"

"Kyra's alibi is strong. She was driving down from Logan Airport when Megan was killed. And so far, there is no DNA evidence that she's involved. Nor is their proof she knew Megan before discovering her body."

"That's not what I was told." Barney's eyes flared open then narrowed, suspicion radiated across his face.

Tom groaned. "Who told you what? Andy? Chief Williams? Or one of their friends sitting on the Council?"

"I—it was in confidence." Barney turned crimson. The sudden flush traveled from his forehead down past his chin. He shook his head, his voice taut. "I won't be put on the spot."

"That's not my intention." Tom pushed an egg around on his plate with a fork. The hunger he'd felt at the police station after his two cup coffee breakfast was gone. He tried keeping his voice calm, but he was too upset. He thought he had handled small town politics rather well since arriving on the Cape—until now. "Don't become part of a conspiracy, Barney. At the end, it'll bite you in the ass."

"That's not fair, Tom. The first time I don't agree with you I'm part of a conspiracy."

"What were you told that you can't repeat? My God, I'm in charge of the investigation."

"Of course, but sometimes people confide in me because I'm the Mayor."

"No problem, except when the info withheld is evidence in a murder case."

"Perhaps you're too close to the suspect?"

"Bullshit! You were given erroneous facts so you would get me to back down." Tight—lipped, he leaned forward. "You know, that will never happen. Why are you hesitant to tell me who and what? I wouldn't cause you harm."

"You don't get it. I'm your staunchest ally, but..." Barney's voice trailed off. "There are people involved I know all my life. Let me see, if I can find anything to substantiate what they said."

"Sounds like you want to do my job. Head the investigation."

Barney gave an awkward, halfhearted chuckle, "I have to do this my way." He reached across the table and extended his hand.

Tom clasped tight. Barney had struck a nerve, and worry welled up inside him. Desperate people were out there. Tom hoped—to—God his brother-in-law didn't ask the wrong people the wrong question. Barney wasn't just the Mayor he was family.

"Hey! We didn't have our second cup of coffee." Barney signaled for the waitress, anxiety creased his brow.

Tom pushed his plate to the side. "These days it seems everyone wants me to go their way. Imagine if we played together as a team. We might solve this crime quicker."

Barney scowled.

"How about it?" Tom offered accidentally biting the inside of his mouth grimacing.

"I'm not repeating anything." Barney looked Tom in the eye. "Until, I check out what I was told."

—⊰+⊱—

Setting up her laptop on the kitchen table, Kyra attempted to update her day's agenda, but she could not get any further than bringing up the original schedule. All she could think of was this morning's headlines and her name on Page One. She hoped JE didn't subscribe to the Cape's daily newspaper.

A sudden knock on the kitchen door and she flipped the computer top closed. Wondering who was out and about so early, she held her breath as the knock became more insistent. Quickly, she glanced out the window, and saw a stocky, brown haired woman who was now banging the brass knocker, calling, "Ms. Stevens, Ms. Stevens."

Who was this woman? Maybe, a reporter? Then why didn't she use the front door? Kyra tucked her cellphones in her pocket and leaving the chain in place, opened the door an inch or two.

"Yes?"

"I'm Mrs. Nelson," the woman said patting her wind swept bobbed hair with French manicured nails.

Taken back by the woman's presence after not hearing from her in a week, Kyra felt the muscles in her neck tighten. "I'm so glad to finally meet you. Come in. I'm Kyra Stevens. We spoke over the telephone several times when I was in Florida."

Unlocking the chain, Kyra swung the door wide and sidestepped. "What ever happened last Monday? I never heard from you and was worried."

"Didn't you get my e-mail?"

"No," Kyra said.

"I don't understand why not. Anyway, my daughter is pregnant. She wasn't feeling very well and the Doctor put her on bed rest. She has a four year old, so I left immediately for Connecticut. I didn't return until last night."

"Did Lieutenant Braden reach you?"

"He called several days ago. I explained what happened and he said not to be concerned, but I should call and stop in when I came back."

Mrs. Nelson appeared well rested, flashed a large multi-stone ring on her right hand and walked to the hall closet to put away her tote and jacket. Her cheeks were bright red from the wind and she glanced into a hall mirror to fix her hair.

Through the front window, Kyra could see a black SUV parked in the turn—around. A kernel of doubt fluttered in her stomach. Several questions played hopscotch in her mind including why Tom didn't tell her he spoke to the housekeeper, but knew she expected too much. "How come you didn't let yourself in?" she said.

"I thought you might have a friend staying overnight."

"That wouldn't cause a problem." Kyra gave a wide smile, wondering why the housekeeper would make such a statement. "But we should set-up a schedule for the next three months."

"Oh," Mrs. Nelson said with surprise. "I thought your visit was just for a month or so."

"Will this cause any difficulties?" Kyra remembered JE's personal assistant, Eva saying the housekeeper wanted more hours.

"Absolutely not." Mrs. Nelson took a bucket of cleaning supplies out of the closet and moved toward the dining room. But she took only a few steps when she stopped short eyeing the yellow crime scene tape. "I thought…"

"I'll ask the police when you can go in. Were you working in the dining room when your daughter phoned."

"Yes," she nodded her head. "I already changed the linen and towels upstairs, didn't think you would entertain as soon as you arrived, so I left everything out on the table."

"Did you happen to see Mrs. McDermott before you left?"

"No." Mrs. Nelson hesitated… "But the Lieutenant said I shouldn't discuss it. He also said that a service company cleaned up the blood. It looks like they did a good job."

"Yes, excellent," Kyra remarked dryly.

⟨⟩

Tom's cell sounded as he slid into his car. Grabbing the phone on the second ring, his muscles tightened as Kyra's name came up. "Hi. I missed you earlier this morning," he said speaking first. "Where were you?"

"At the library."

"The library?"

"Just gathering info. Whales Bay is a really nice town. I'm reading up on its history and founders. The Dickerson and McDermott families seemed to have run everything for over the last one hundred years. But outside of Andy McDermott, all of them seemed to have disappeared."

A chill shot through him. What was she up to? "Is this in preparation for your company to buy the entire coastline?" He heard her chuckle—loud and clear.

"I love history," she replied in an innocent tone. "Oh, and Mrs. Nelson dropped in. Said the two of you spoke."

"Why did you call?" He asked ignoring her comments.

"It's lobster night. How about coming over? Perhaps you could fill me in on your conversation with the housekeeper."

Surprised at the unexpected invitation so soon, Tom hesitated.

"You're due," Kyra continued. "Home—cooked dinner, quid—pro—quo, share the history, not the murder. Remember? I still play Chef."

"How could I forget?" Nor could he forget that he held her, kissed her. She seemed to forget the night of the storm and their moment, as she called it.

"I would love too, but I can't make it tonight. Matt has a Little League game. Sorry." He really was.

She paused for the briefest of moments, and then murmured, "I haven't been to a Little League game in years."

He heard the wistfulness in her voice.

"I'd love to go—meet Matt. And, we can't have you reneging on our deal, so, my treat afterwards, pizza or hamburgers? Let's make it Matt's choice."

"Fast foods don't count in our arrangement, Kyra. Remember, a home cooked meal." He chuckled. "I'm not reneging. Just have to renegotiate. About tonight, I don't think—don't want Matt hearing murder stories…"

She cut him off. "Give me a break, Tom. I have several nephews and a niece. I would never say a …" her voice trailed off.

He listened to silence, nothing, not even her breathing, "Kyra?"

No answer.

"Kyra," he shouted into the cell fear slicing through him.

"I'm sorry. Didn't think."

Her voice so low, he pressed the phone tight against his ear.

"He—you—might be going with friends. I don't want to intrude. After all, I am the number one suspect in town." She exhaled deeply. "If you want, the next time it's—spaghetti night," her voice grew louder, "Please, bring Matt." She clicked off.

"Kyra, don't hang up." Damn! He brought up her number; hit it. "We'll pick you up at six."

━┽┼┾━

Kyra paced behind the catcher at home plate, hands thrust deep into the pockets of her powder blue anorak. To the umpire's dismay, she had climbed out of the stands two innings ago, heckling several of his calls.

She was not happy the coach had taken the centerfielder out of the game; and even less happy with the way he favored better players, or the way the game was going.

"Tell your friend to calm down," Pete's dad said, chuckling from the sidelines. A short, wiry man, his son was built like him, and pitched for the opposing team.

"She tells it like it is," Tom muttered, climbing out of the stands and joining Kyra, as Matt came up to bat.

Seventh inning, one out, one on first base, Tom cringed for his son, felt his nervousness.

The coach called time out, walked over to home plate whispered in the boy's ear and strode away; arms crossed over his chest, chewing rapidly.

One strike.

Matt leaned in.

One ball.

"Bunt," Kyra mouthed the word.

"He could get a good one, drive in a run," Tom said. "He's fast as the wind."

"First, he has to connect." Kyra turned towards him. "He's not a strong hitter. Needs practice. But he can bunt. And this play calls for it."

"Did you learn under Joe Torre or Girardi?" For the briefest of moments, he thought a streak of lightening zig—zagged through her eyes.

She eyed him dead—on. He could see she wanted to say more, but she caught her lower lip, swallowed hard. The early evening breeze blew tendrils about her face; her cheeks had turned apple red. He didn't know if he wanted to touch or nibble on them.

"I did better than that. My father made sure his daughter played Little League, and did as well as his sons. I spent hours in the batting cage and covering second base on the field." She turned back to the game. "Give it all you got, Matt," she shouted.

Fowl! Two strikes and three balls!

The coach called time again, walked out to home base. Matt looked miserable.

He's going to hit into a double play, Tom worried, his chest tightening in advance for his son's disappointment.

"Sacrifice. Bunt. The kid can do it. Stop making him nervous," she mumbled at the coach. Turning half way to Tom, she said, "That guy shouldn't be working with the younger teams."

"Double play!"

Matt walked back to his teammates. Tom hurt for his son. A swell of verbal sympathy flowed across the field.

"Great try," Kyra shouted, applauding with Tom and several other parents who had joined in.

"You know, not everyone is cut out to be another Mickey Mantle," Tom said.

"True, but everyone can try there hardest. You said he ran like the wind. That's his big asset. His potential is to prove it by practicing on his hitting and getting on base."

"You are tenacious, aren't you?" Probably, what drove her to the top of the corporate ladder? Made her what she is.

Kyra pursed her lips, climbed to their seats on the second row with the grace of a ballerina.

Tom watched, troubled, and followed. A fire burned inside her. He could see it, feel it. He didn't know if he could put it out, or if anyone should?

Pete's dad did a sudden double take. His eyes pasted to Kyra's face.

But she was focused on Matt's team taking the field. Only, Matt wasn't running out. "Shit," she said looking around.

His son sat hunched up against the schoolyard, metal fence alongside several other kids. A number of them had struck out earlier.

Tom grinded his teeth, pressed his thumb down hard on his pager that had just gone off, not looking at the text. Planning what he could say to his son that would ease the hurt, build his confidence.

"You know I have some time, in the late afternoons," Kyra said glancing from the pager to Tom's face. "I'd love to practice with Matt." She looked as earnest as all hell. "I'm good, really. Assistant Coach on my youngest brother's team. We'll have fun, I promise. And, if you're around..." she shrugged.

He believed her, but would Chief Williams? And would it acerbate the situation with Barney. Set her up for a fall.

What was he thinking, anyway? Having her coach Matt? Would he be right in fostering a relationship for his son with a murder suspect? The two seemed to have hit it off on the drive over. But Kyra was also his first female friend that had interacted with his son.

And of course, there was the Assistant District Attorney who would jump to prosecute the case? Pete's dad had turned milk white after recognizing Kyra. Thick brows rose in question marks, as he tilted his head at her. His whiskey colored eyes shot Tom a belligerent look.

Tom pretended not to notice. At this point, it was none of the man's business, anyway. The case hadn't been pushed upstairs; and he refused to jump on the get—Kyra—bandwagon. Professionally, he believed her innocent. Personally, she touched his heart.

CHAPTER EIGHT

The next morning, Kyra's smart phone informed her that six messages were waiting. She tapped in her code and the operator announced the first was from James Enrico. So was the second, third and fourth. Why bother looking at the fifth and sixth that were labeled Private Caller? Probably his, too! For unknown reasons, the CEO would switch from one smart phone to another, depending on his mood.

The timber of his voice escalated in each of the four calls as he announced his name and title.

Did he really think she forgot who he was and whom she worked for?

She punched the speed-dial number reserved by JE just for her.

He picked up on the first ring. "Ah, almost time for brunch. And you, Kyrita—having a late morning coffee? I thought you forgot why I sent you to the Cape. You know, how I worry day and night. I had to ask myself, why would she let me suffer unnecessarily?"

"Meetings, so many. The New Englanders can be so tough." Her mind zipped over the previous day's events pulling out the bits and pieces she could ignore and those she should divulge. But first, she waited to hear if his tone lightened.

A dusting of amusement did coat his words, "Alesandro thought the flight wore you out and you finally had to catch up on your sleep."

"Alesandro was wrong," she said and thought *I had an exciting evening with a sexy man and his delightful son.*

"H'mm, sometimes Alesandro is wrong, but not often. So I wondered," his voice, silky as one of his five hundred dollar bottles of wine, "Has my Kyrita met a man?"

She chuckled flaunting her southern lilt. "Difficult to think about men when all one is concentrating on is a billion dollar deal."

"Si, Kyrita, how very true."

She knew how he worried. And it had nothing to do with her meeting a man, unless James Enrico felt the impact would affect her job performance. Otherwise, he seemed to take an almost paternal interest in the few dinner engagements that never went anywhere; and the cocktail parties where she was seen.

But her sleeping the day away was a company no—no, and a cause for grave disappointment, especially now, when she was closing in on a beautiful coastline and interested investors anxious to be included in a Harbors Conglomerate venture.

Ah yes, Alesandro. The gentle giant had struck again with his little homily uttered only for James Enrico's ears. *That one was yours, my colleague, but the next one will be mine.*

With brow furrowed, she adopted a conspiratorial tone, "I hired a boat. Took it out, steered it myself. Up and down the coastline, surveying the shore and the beaches." She felt guilty as the words slipped out of her mouth, but she would make it right by covering them with the truth. "I'll be going out again within the week." She couldn't postpone any longer. It was on her original itinerary since the trip was planned.

"And you will shoot photos?" A flicker of happiness flavored James Enrico's words.

"Of course, just as we discussed, tons of them, with my digital camera. You'll feel as if you were standing beside me on the boat." She hoped he was mollified. Otherwise, this inane conversation could go on for hours.

"And you'll attach the file of photos, e-mail them immediately."

"As soon as I return from the dock."

"Si, Kyrita." He ended with, "Please call, more timely. Worrying isn't good for anyone."

She clicked off. A slow chill traveled through her body. Why was JE being so obvious? She would love to feed him a line. Make up for his throwaway remark about Biloxi. She spent hours searching the Internet for a Harbors and Biloxi connection and couldn't find a single one. Not even e-mail from her staff. With deliberation he tormented her.

She would have liked to say—it was a man. That's the reason I didn't telephone. But he would gamble—ask—if it was the homicide Lieutenant. And her little joke could evolve into a quagmire. One of the first things she learned when she started working for JEC Industries was that James Enrico only loved jokes when they were his.

She pressed the end button, went to delete the fifth message then changed her mind. Might as well listen, she decided, in case JE used another one of his phones to add a few additional words of wisdom.

A woman's voice sounded in her ear. "I—I'm sorry. Do I have the right number? I'm looking for Kyra Stevens. It's Lilly Brewster. I work in Town Hall. The Records Department. If you would please return my call, it's very important."

Wondering, if the call had anything to do with Chief Williams, Kyra pressed send. She hoped she didn't cause a problem for the young woman. "Good morning, Lilly," she said, at the click of the receiver.

"Good Morning, we met the other day in Town Hall."

"Of course. Lilly; the wealth of information," Kyra said smiling. "What's up?"

"I don't know how to say this, but…" her voice trailed off. "Last night, a friend called." She hesitated, voice strained. "And…"

"And?" Kyra repeated. The little hairs on the back of her neck stood up. Was the Chief of Police or the Lieutenant the friend?

"She wanted to know about you. What kind of person you were?"

"What kind…? A Woman? What is your friend's name?"

"Victoria—Victoria Dickinson."

Kyra paused a heartbeat. "Where does she live?" Ellridge said there weren't any Dickinson's from the original founding fathers living in Massachusetts. Perhaps a distant relative or two. Maybe several scattered across the country none of which had anything to do with the trust. Set up years ago, the original estate was almost broke and the trustees needed to sell the beachfront property.

"Victoria lives in Boston."

What was going on? Wrong information. Her research people were the best, very rare for them to get their facts wrong.

Ellridge claimed he double—checked their info and it was correct. "Exactly what did Ms. Dickinson ask?" Kyra said. "And is she a close friend, or an acquaintance?"

"Oh no," Lilly gave a slight chuckle. "She grew up with my grandmother. They were childhood friends."

"Your grandmother and Victoria Dickinson!"

"Yes."

"And Ms. Dickinson wanted to know what kind of person I was?"

"Yes."

"Did she tell you why?"

"Well, this is where it gets complicated." Lilly heaved a deep sigh. "She's quite elderly; eighty-seven. Not in the best of health and she was very upset. That's the reason why I'm calling."

"Okay." Kyra's pulse rate started to rise. A cramp was making its way into her gut.

"She said you telephoned several times offering to buy the old Dickinson estate. That you would phone as soon as you arrived from Florida and settled in." Lilly paused. "But you never called. Then she read about the murder," her voice grew lower. "Kyra, Victoria's quite perturbed that she is doing business with a—a killer."

"I can imagine," Kyra murmured. "Considering that I'm the Chief of Police's primary person of interest whose name is all over the media."

Dead silence.

"Lilly, I'm sorry, but Chief Williams does like his publicity."

No response.

"Lilly, are you there?" Kyra, be quiet. Use your head. She works down the hall from the Police Chief. You're a stranger, and she's young, perhaps not experienced in matters of one—up—man—ship.

"So—it's not true?" Lilly said a flicker of hope in her tone.

"That I'm the murderer? Yes. I wasn't on the Cape when Mrs. McDermott was killed. I just found her body."

Nor did I ever speak to your friend, she added to herself. Silent for a moment, she went on, "I'd like to meet Ms. Dickinson. Straighten things out. Can you arrange it?"

"Of course," Lilly's voice perked up.

"We can drive to Boston together? Perhaps have lunch with Victoria."

"She would like that very much." Lilly sounded as if a weight was lifted from her chest.

Did Victoria ask the young woman to telephone, arrange to meet? But how was she aware her best friend's granddaughter, Lilly, knew Kyra Stevens, the knife—slasher.

A dozen different ways! Don't harp on it, now. Just get up there and find out who is impersonating you?

"I'm off tomorrow," Lilly said.

"Great. I'm free, too. Give me your address and I'll pick you up around ten." Thank God, she told JE, she would take the offshore pictures within the week and not the next day.

She jotted down directions, said good-bye, and then sat listening to the dial tone in a state of despair. Her vacation—slash—business trip felt more like a due—diligence audit hunting down illicit information rather than setting up the venture for a condo and hotel resort. The one thing she could always count on was her resources back at corporate. Now, even that seemed to be sliding across thin ice. Automatically, she picked up the last call.

<u>"You can run, but you can't hide. I'll be back. Sooner than you think."</u>

Kyra dropped the phone. Rubbed the side of her neck gasped for air!

She heard a noise in the front of the house, got up, hurried down the hall and peered through the front bay window. A police car was driving up the circular drive. The car stopped and the officer got out to scan the house. Seeing Kyra hold back the curtain, he waved. She waved back watching as he returned to his car and drove off.

Just like Tom told her last night at the game, Whales Bay's periodic check. When he said it, she felt safe. In reality, she knew there were several hours between now and the next drive through. Plenty of time for her stalker to call again circle her house and break in with his weapon of choice. A knife. A Maglite. Whatever was handy?

The phone rang, a spurt of fear zoomed through her.

"Good morning," Tom's voice filled her with joy and guilt. "How are you doing?"

"Great," she said. "And I had a wonderful evening at the game. Thank you for the invite."

"Any time. Something has come up and I have to go over a few things. Can you stop in at my office this morning?"

"Of course!"

"In an hour."

"Can't wait," she said and realized, she meant it.

The desk Sargent directed her to Tom's office and as she passed the squad room, he called her name.

She spun around. He was quickly walking toward her flashing a wide smile. Even his stride sent a hot cramp into her groin. A short breath caught in her throat. This wasn't good. Get a grip.

"I got the Chief to listen," he announced as he caught up.

"Then Williams is issuing a statement that I'm not a person of interest?"

"Not exactly. He placed a hand on her elbow steered her two doors down, motioned to a visitor's chair. "The Chief claims he never stated anything so obvious in the newspapers or on TV."

"But...

"He will speak to several reporters to cool down the rhetoric."

"His picture was on Page One with my name. And so were his remarks."

"He doesn't agree. Claims you're interpreting the reporter's words, who wants to sell extra newspapers, and your situation to publicize your company's intentions in building their resort."

"My situation. What about the Chiefs situation to grab headlines? You even said..."

"He and I were two cops reviewing different scenarios. I shouldn't have mentioned it."

"What?"

"It's mostly innuendo and he intends to call the reporters on it."

"And you don't understand that the way Williams is handling this investigation can cause irreversible harm to my position on the company's executive board." Her gut shouted, if you knew who was waiting for me to stumble? "I could lose the Harbors project before it got off the ground."

Standing, she looked directly at him. "Maybe I should get a lawyer." She felt like a herd of horses were bearing down on her. But, she was still erect.

She swung her tote bag over a shoulder and brushed past, barely got the words out of her mouth. "I'm driving up to Boston, tomorrow."

His eyes held her gaze and for the briefest of moments she was without a thought in her head, feeling completely connected, but the rational part of her brain said the attraction was only in her mind. It was not two sided.

Her smart phone sang.

Tom gave a quick nod towards her purse.

A remnant of fear from her previous frightening call earlier made her nervous to pick up. She fished in her pocket book to delay answering. Wanted to be outside, alone, not in front of him.

Tom frowned.

The ringing stopped.

She shrugged. "No patience." Thankfully, she took a step to the door.

The ringing started again.

"What's wrong, Kyra?" Tom's voice deep, questioning. He reached out circled her arm with his hand. If she told him about her earlier message, he would try to talk her out of driving to Boston.

She had no choice, but to grab the cell, and talk.

"Hi Sweetie, thought I had the wrong number." Charlie's voice warmed her insides.

"My brother." She smiled.

Tom relaxed. The nerve stopped beating. He let go of her arm, but a question mark clouded his eyes.

"You're not alone?" Charlie asked.

"I'm meeting with a police lieutenant."

"Braden? The news is all over our office."

"Please don't tell me the Florida media has the story." She glared at Tom.

"No. The FBI. You've made the big time, Kyra. Do you need me?"

"Not yet," she hesitated. The newspapers would have a field day, the FBI versus the Cape Cod Police. Would James Enrico ask her to return? Alesandro would love to visit New England.

She swallowed hard.

"I've got personal time. No problem," Charlie added. "I could even bring company."

"I'll let you know. How are Mom and Dad?"

"Great. Thinking of taking a trip to New York, next month. Might even drive up to the Cape."

They laughed together. "They don't know, do they?"

"Not that I'm aware of."

Otherwise, she thought, her father would be flying up today. She had stopped him from running interference after Miami. But the lawyer in him eventually came out.

"Go back to your meeting. Stay in touch. Don't forget a strong offense always wins."

A chuckle rose within her as she tapped the phone off and dropped it in her bag. Leave it to Charlie. Still playing one—on—one on the basketball court.

"What's so funny?" Tom asked.

"He—my brother, Charlie tends to simplify things." Her eye locked again with his. "This case has blown completely out of proportion. Charlie heard about it. He lives and works in Florida." She swallowed hard. "Your Chief Williams has caused irrevocable damage to my reputation."

"Have you received any other calls?" his tone demanded. He ignored her comments, seemed to be reading her thoughts.

"At this particular moment I have nothing to say," she hissed and stalked out of police headquarters.

CHAPTER NINE

The next day, Kyra and Lilly arrived under a high golden sun at Victoria Dickenson's brownstone. A well-endowed housekeeper escorted them into the living room. The house smelled deliciously of hot cinnamon and aromatic tea.

Victoria's blue eyes sparkled seeing Lilly and she smothered her in a hug then smoothed her blond curls back from her face.

Kyra was greeted with a firm handshake and an inquisitive expression. "From your voice, I didn't realize you were so young and pretty."

"From my voice?" Kyra repeated.

"Yes. You sounded about twenty years older on the telephone and I didn't detect a southern dialect, more of a New England one. Voices tell a great deal about people."

"Interesting," Kyra murmured, wondering whom she knew that was older, not from the south, but informed about the planned hotel on the Cape.

She sat quietly in the corner of the burgundy brocaded sofa, looking around, not paying attention to the two women playing catch up.

Exquisite antiques dotted the room. The floor was covered with thick beige carpeting and long sheer beige curtains were pulled up out of the way to allow most of the natural light to stream in.

The housekeeper returned rolling a silver service for tea and a platter of homemade French fruit tarts. Victoria poured the tea, offered the pastries, abstaining from taking either. She locked eyes with Kyra; spoke with a broad Bostonian accent. "Lilly explained that you discovered Megan's body and weren't on the Cape when she was killed. Then why are you the main suspect in the murder?"

"That's what I keep asking the police, but they ignore my questions."

"They might have evidence that keeps you in the mix, so they are unable to remove you from their list of suspects."

"That is impossible. As Lilly told you, I was driving down from Logan Airport when Megan was killed. I never was on the Cape before, or met any of the people involved in the case."

A cold wave of apprehension touched every nerve in her body. Victoria Dickenson didn't seem to be sickly or feeble. Instead, sharp and keen. If Victoria was confused about the newspaper articles, so was she. And if the lady said she spoke to Kyra Stevens, then someone definitely phoned using her name. Kyra felt as if something was crawling across her skin in this elegant house on the hill.

A regal grandfather clock ticked each second on the other side of the room. The older woman's eyes roamed from Kyra's French braid down to her high—heel ankle boots. For some inane reason, Kyra hoped she passed inspection.

Knowing they were waiting for her to begin, she took a deep breath speaking in a soft tone, not wanting to upset either woman.

She handed them her business cards and paused while they read them before speaking. "I'm the Vice-President of Acquisitions for JEC Industries. We are interested in the beachfront Dickerson property in Whales Bay. However, I did not call previously and have no idea who did. I think the best thing is to start as if this was our first discussion."

"Why would anyone do such a thing?" Victoria gasped.

"I can only suppose, and that is meaningless. But I would like to know if you own the property, or does the Dickerson Estate hold the title?"

"I am the Dickerson estate and the other woman asked the same question. James Arnold Dickerson was my Great—great grandfather. I have a Grand—niece Mary who lives in Virginia and there is my Grand-nephew Robert, both of whom have minor shares."

Kyra plastered a half-smile onto her face and tried to control her shaky voice. "Did the other woman ask where Robert lives?"

"No she didn't. But he lives in Whales Bay. Maybe you met him? He's the Mayor and owns Barneys, a great restaurant. Third generation."

Kyra's heart dropped to her ankles.

After a light lunch, Lilly and Victoria wanted to make a few stops and do some shopping. Kyra explained she had to drop something off at a business acquaintance and would pick-up Lilly in an hour. Saying her goodbyes to Victoria, she promised to call within the next few days.

Following her GPS, Kyra pulled into the underground parking lot in less than fifteen minutes. As She took the elevator to the top floor—the twelfth—Kyra wondered if the same woman who impersonated her on the telephone with Victoria also did so when she called Megan McDermott as Andy had insisted. If this was true, who was the woman?

The elevator stopped and opened into a reception foyer.

Lawrence Ellridge's secretary, very tall and very elegant in a tailored ensemble, led Kyra into his office announced her name, and closed the door.

The lawyer dominated the room standing erect and somber in front of the four-foot high oil paintings of what appeared to be his father, grandfather and great-grandfather. He rested one hand on the arm of his burgundy, leather executive chair. "Wasn't necessary to drive up to Boston, Kyra. I was scheduled to be in Whales Bay, tomorrow."

A flash of Deja Vu instantly struck her. Lawrence approaching her table in the restaurant, wearing a similar if not the same expensive, three piece suit, speaking without a greeting, as if he was continuing an ongoing conversation from a previous time.

He motioned to a visitor's chair, "Please. Would you like something to drink?" He sat down, picked up a gold, Mont Blanc pen and rolled it between his fingers.

"No, thank you." She crossed her legs, attempted to catch his gaze, but Lawrence's eyes focused somewhere between the pen and her forehead. "I felt the matter couldn't wait."

She found it difficult picturing this man in a courtroom; hard looking with a mean mouth. A jury would think too formidable; that they and his client didn't matter. He presented evidence and everyone was supposed to pay his or her utmost attention to his words and believe him.

The same would pertain to board meetings. She had a distinct feeling that around a conference table Lawrence oozed his importance; would not participate in a give—or—take discussion. He would have no inclination to meet on common ground. The Ellridge way—or nothing at all! What she first thought of, as animosity toward her, now seemed just his typical day—to—day personality.

Cool it Kyra, you're not here to psychoanalyze him.

"What is so important?" he asked.

Not the barest of apologies for keeping her waiting a half hour even after his secretary had confirmed their appointment and reiterated Lawrence's propensity for punctuality. For someone so time conscious this was the second time in five days he kept her waiting.

But now, Lilly would be waiting and she didn't want to inconvenience the young woman. Kyra felt she had to get to the point and leave without pressing any other issues.

"I have to review where we stand on several of the properties."

"Such as?"

"The old Whales Bay town beach and the Dickinson estate that adjoins it." She folded her hands in her lap studying his face.

His rigid shoulders stiffened even more and he stared at her over silver—rimmed eyeglasses perched on the tip of his nose. "Why?"

"I need the information for a report." How long did he think she would play Trivia Pursuit?

"To whom?"

"Don't bother yourself with whom," she said in a cold, detached monotone. "Let's start. I have other appointments in the city that I'm now late for." Hopefully, it would all work out. To someone with Lawrence's personality, her previous remark wouldn't rest well. Not caring, she glared across the desk.

He reached for the top manila folder perched on a small multi—colored group to his left. "I haven't started negotiations with the town. Just put feelers out." He centered the file in the middle of his desk, adjusted the corners and clasped his hands on top without opening it.

"Do these feelers take into consideration the town's plans for the property?"

"It's been lying dormant for years," he annunciated in his officious voice.

"I understand another developer is interested."

"Have no idea where you got that information." A perturbed expression creased his face and accented his tone.

"It'll jack up our costs, if we're caught in a bidding war," she continued. "I can't express how important this is."

"Again, I repeat, I have no idea what you are talking about."

She knew he was lying, but why? As she said to Victoria she could speculate, but it wouldn't mean anything. She needed the

93

truth, so she wouldn't fail. "Then I suggest you investigate and re-port back to me as soon as possible." She riveted her eyes with his. He glared back. She definitely could picture him with a knife in his hands and she stiffened.

"What about the Dickinson estate?" She drew herself up wait-ing for the story he was going to hand her about the most important piece of land in the puzzle?

"That's more difficult," he gave a sarcastic glance, adjusted his glasses and opened the file. "You never ask for anything easy."

She bit the inside of her lip. "That's why I hired someone of your caliber." But I didn't know the games you played and the lies you told. The words boomeranged in her head.

He gave a slight chuckle.

Surprised, she waited. He could save or sink the relationship with his next words.

"Dickinson is such a common name. Sometimes it feels as if we're falling all over them. Other times it feels as if the particular branch of the family we're seeking—is gone."

"Gone?" The word stuck in her throat. She hoped the amaze-ment she felt didn't show on her face. So what, if it did?

He skimmed over several pages. "We had several good leads, but they didn't pan out: tenth cousin of the Great-grandfather's son—in—law, or some other nonsense. People written out of prior Wills." He dismissed the entire idea with a wave of his hand.

She gave a quick glance at his family oil portraits. Ellridge ob-viously didn't feel such relationships were nonsense when they per-tained to his ancestors.

"None locally?" She tried pinning him down. Afraid he would lie, a part of her did not want him too. It would create additional obstacles with JE.

"I told you we couldn't find anyone from the James Arnold Dickerson family tree. Especially, living in New England. Nothing has changed."

They locked eyes. She became aware of a tiny flicker behind his glasses and recognized he now suspected she was interfering in what he thought was his sole domain.

"I can expect updates of any changes after you investigate?"

"That goes without saying."

In her heart, she knew she would never trust him. She had too much information at her finger—tips that proved otherwise. Among which was that Victoria Dickerson's Boston townhouse was not more than one mile from Ellridge's office. Victoria's name and status plus her location should have made her a well-known entity to Mr. Ellridge.

It was at that moment, Kyra decided she would not jeopardize Lilly's position, nor bring Victoria Dickinson's name into the mix until it was absolutely necessary. There had to be another way to introduce her information to James Enrico without damaging the young woman's job, or Victoria's plans.

She just had to figure it out.

CHAPTER TEN

C louds drifted over the ocean as Kyra turned down the rutted lane and a marina sprang into view. She slowed, parking next to a small brashly painted shanty with its posted rental fees.

She smelled the sea air, heard the gulls squawking as first they circled above and then dove for fish below the water's surface.

Further out, one hearty soul braved the choppy waves swimming parallel to the shore. A few sailboats dotted the horizon and she had a quick flash of other times and different beaches.

She shook her head trying to dismiss the flood of memories that came rushing in. The endless hours she spent sailing with her three brothers, Dennis, Charlie and Josh.

Now, a favorite pastime would become a skill—surveying the shoreline—where Harbors planned on building their new resort.

Locking the car, Kyra glanced around. The marina appeared deserted except for the lone man who was helping a young couple, bundled in life preservers, maneuver a small powerboat away from the dock. "Hi there," she called.

"Be with you in a minute." Giving her a slight nod, the man pushed the boat off. "Now, a good yank," he shouted.

The guy in the vest pulled back on the lanyard and the boat took off shooting a spray in its wake.

The man turned towards her, burly, middle-aged with a weather beaten face and hands. "How can I help?"

"I'd like to rent a power boat for several hours, but I want something bigger." She flourished a hand toward the one puttering away from the dock. "And faster. Do you have a Searay?"

"Are you alone?" he asked in a thick smoker's voice.

"Yes."

Surprise crinkling his brow, the man eyed her up and down. "Have you handled one before?"

"I grew up on the Outer Banks. My brothers and I powered a boat, as much as we drove a car."

Hesitant, the man pointed to a sleek red and white berthed further down the pier.

Kyra beamed with approval, strode over for a closer view. "Nice. It'll do fine."

The man held open the shanty door. A blue carved sign showing a captain's hat with the name Vince painted on the brim hung behind the counter. "Got a cell phone? In case you have to call for help."

She couldn't decide if he was being factious or just cautious. With a slight chuckle, she patted the leather phone case clipped to the waistband of her jeans. "Don't worry. And I'm certified." She rattled off both her certificate and phone numbers.

Unimpressed, the man processed her paperwork.

When she handed him a credit card, and he compared it to her driver's license, he suddenly stopped. Stone faced, he drew in a sharp breath. "I thought so. You're the one who found Megan McDermott's body?"

"I—yes, I am." She held his gaze. "A terrible tragedy."

He snorted, watched her sign the receipt. Then expressionless, he slid her credit card back across the counter. Red—rimmed hazel eyes roved—searching—from her shoulder strap bag, along her sweatshirt and down to her jeans lingering at each pocket.

My God, she realized, he thinks I'm hiding something that I intend to drop over board. Gritting her teeth, she put away the wallet, and head held high walked to the boat. No one, no one was going to intimidate her.

Her anger grew with each step she took at the way the police had dragged her into their investigation with its accompanying notoriety. Why?

All she did was find a dead woman and report it like a good citizen. In Miami, things had gone smoother. But then—down there—everything went smoother. People bent backwards for a Harbors Vice President.

The clouds were dissipating and the sun felt warm on her face. She concentrated on the dashboard, ignoring the seething man on the wharf who was—watching—testing her boat expertise, or perhaps how far she could throw a knife.

Little did he know, she had been tested by many other experienced people; her father for one, who insisted only on perfection, the sailing academy that she and her brothers had to graduate before they could operate a boat on their own.

A car door slamming shut broke through her reverie. Ignoring it, she concentrated on the controls.

From the corner of her eye, she could see Vince wasn't interested in who pulled up. He continued to squint in her direction.

Someone jogged along the moving fingers of the wharf.

Vince didn't move a muscle.

Kyra reached to turn the key, just as someone jumped on board.

"Who?" she exclaimed! And swerved around. "What are you doing here?" She glared at Tom, winced at her tone and the words that had tumbled, so mean, out of her mouth.

But yesterday, learning that Barney was a Dickerson was too much to ignore. Putting that together with Tom's defense of Chief Williams had placed her in a very suspicious mode.

Though Kyra had to admit, she never told Tom about her interest in the Dickerson founding family, their descendants, or their land. And she couldn't recall any one mentioning Barney's last name. She swallowed hard. Tried to control her senses and not blow things out of proportion.

"I'm touched by your welcome. Good morning would have been sufficient," Tom said.

"Why, are you here?" Kyra demanded. "Did you follow me? I don't remember extending an invitation."

"But I knew you wanted too. And I didn't follow." His grin slid across his mouth. Anger was etched in the corners of his eyes reflecting the green of the ocean that rocked the boat. His shirtsleeves rolled up, collar and shirt halfway unbuttoned, one lone curl tumbling across his forehead, body language—ready to pounce.

On her?

A hot wave of desire coursed through her.

She recalled the few fleeting times when she was positive he wanted her, as much as she wanted him. And her nerves even tingled now, as they spoke.

The sun was rising higher and higher in the sky. She went from hot to cold and back again, her nipples hardening, pressing, against her tee shirt under the sweatshirt. She hadn't bothered putting on a bra, today. Not expecting company, but here he was.

Off to the side, Kyra could see Vince still standing on the dock rolling up a large pile of rope. Probably, transfixed by the interaction between her and the Lieutenant. Hoping that he would be a witness to her being handcuffed, arrested and hauled away.

She felt exposed to the elements; vulnerable to this man who excited her very being and seemed to invade every place she went.

"Why did you take off without letting anyone know where you were going?"

"I didn't realize I had too."

"You disappeared yesterday."

"In your office, I mentioned that I had an appointment in Boston."

"And today, you left before the sun came up. A Whales Bay patrol car tagged along until they were dispatched to an accident. Williams wants to know what's going on. His men reported it was the second day you couldn't be found."

"As I said previously, yesterday I went to Boston. I returned late afternoon, and was home all night in Whales Bay. If anyone was that interested in my whereabouts, they could have knocked on the door. And today, I'm vacationing on your beautiful shore."

"The Chief was ready to search the estate again, and cancel the drive—bys."

"What stopped him?"

"CSI reported there were traces that someone had been casing your place."

She didn't know if it was his tone, or what he'd said that sent the fear escalating up into her chest and throat.

"What traces?"

"We found several pairs of muddy footprints and seaweed. It appears you had two intruders on several occasions."

"Seaweed?" she questioned.

Tom moved towards her, his broad shoulders blocking out the sun, the wind rippling through his hair fanning out like one of those half—naked, dashing men in a magazine advertisement. Shadows flickered across his face; high cheekbones, jaw set. He was so strong, so sure of himself. Was he as sure of her, or was she his enigma?

"Then I don't understand." She compressed her lips, her voice tight with frustration. "Someone is out to get me, or get into the house, but I'm still the Chief of Police's prime suspect."

He leaned toward her. "That's why I'm here. To protect you."

"From who? The police or the killer?"

"I'm on your side, Kyra."

She wanted to believe him, but was afraid too.

"There's no way you could have murdered Megan. The Medical Examiner is emphatic about the time of death. You were driving down from Boston when the killing took place."

"That's what I've been saying all along. Now, your people have given me an alibi." A feeling of relief washed over her. But something still gnawed away at her. Could he be using this case as his big opportunity to prove himself? Or was he working on a land deal with Barney?

She knew more about ambition than most people. And her instincts were reliable. "Are you using me for bait, Lieutenant? Trying to make the big score?"

"I would never put you in harm's way," he said firmly. "But I need your help to find the truth."

She had vowed never to let another man hurt her. Especially, someone she hardly knew—like Tom. But at this very moment, she wanted it to be true; that she tugged at his heart like he tugged at hers.

"How?" she asked.

"For starters, you could compile a list of who would have a reason to kill you."

"We are back to compiling a list!" She still felt appalled at his suggestion. "A list!" she shouted, shaking her head in bewilderment. They were back where they began.

"Perhaps someone who's after your job," Tom added. "Let's start with the bloody business world."

Or perhaps someone who never forgot I was promoted over him? She shuddered—remembering—five years earlier. The memory had haunted her since she found Megan's body in the deserted mansion, Megan's body, which bore such a strong resemblance to her's.

She had failed with the Gaspard advertising campaign that promoted the re—opening of Harbors Houston Resort on the Gulf of Mexico. The highly touted hotel and condo lost millions after suffering damage from Hurricane Ike. It was her first big project that she had to sign off on. Lure the investors and vacationers into returning. But she didn't draw enough of the right people. She didn't reach the big money.

Ignoring the advice spinning around him, James Enrico gave her a larger budget.

And she pulled it off!

From then on, Kyra walked beside JE; sat on his right, was tied to him by beeper and cell day and night. But it was Alessandro's path she walked, Alessandro's seat she sat in.

Then last spring, a sultry afternoon on a Miami patio, over olives and MITIE's, Isabella, James Enrico's lover confided that Alesandro wished her dead.

Balding and kind—faced, the one they called the Gentle Giant, would he have hired a hit man to kill her?

Her stomach rolled over at the thought. She laid her hand on her waist. Patted it softly.

"There is no list. Anyone who wants my job would have to work twenty-four/seven. I don't think he or she would have time to go on a murder spree."

Tom propped one hip against the railing. "Cast-off lovers carry a grudge. Don't forget Gregg. And of course, wives of ex-lovers. They're the worst." He gave her a wry grin. "Any of them around?"

She gaped at him in stunned silence. "I never had that much fun."

A slow burn made its way up into her throat. "Sorry to disappoint you Lieutenant, but that's not my style. Don't confuse me with someone you know."

"We have to ask. It's procedure. I didn't mean…"

She cut him off not wanting to be drawn into a personal conversation. "I arrived after the woman's death to live in the house where she was murdered. That's my connection."

"But what if the killer arrived early and killed Megan thinking it was you?"

Could she be wrong?

Would Tom ever forgive her for withholding information and worse—would she be alive to even know?

For the second time, she reached for the key. She started the motor, engaged the propeller. Tom's presence drew Vince's help—and he pushed the boat off—the motor cutting its way through the waves.

She relished the wind, the sun, and the smell of the salty sea. And she breathed in deep.

How would she be able to take pictures of the shoreline with Lieutenant Braden hovering about? And today, he was definitely—the Lieutenant.

She steered the boat to calmer waters. Her head throbbed. The day might turn out to be a joy ride after all unless she figured how to photograph the site. She would also like to control the emotional turmoil Tom's presence and conversation awoke in her.

She had a full life, good job and friends. She preferred companionship with a lover, not just sex. No casual hookups, no weekend rendezvous in a foreign getaway—she needed relationships.

But she had to admit that for the first time in years this man sent her insides churning, her priorities swirling around aching to switch.

Her father always said, "Set your mind on your goal. Aim—and never take your eyes off the target." However, sex and murder were not factors in his calculations.

This can't go anyplace the little nagging voice suggested in her ear. Remember your agenda!

How could she forget? It was like playing a game of jacks. Bounce the red ball up. Grab the jacks with the other hand. Juggle the two. Only now, she was juggling her career with an emotional need.

"Want me to handle the wheel?" Tom prompted. He had moved to the passenger seat, leaned back, at ease with the world.

"You know how?" she sounded like Vince. Bit her tongue, but what a great idea. Problem solved. "Sorry, I thought you were a city boy."

"I used to spend summers with my grandparents on the Jersey Shore," he smiled contentedly.

"In a little while," she purred. "As soon as we reach the bend, the wheel is yours."

Tom watched Kyra fiddling with the digital camera. She shaded the lens with her left hand for several shots concentrating with a photographer's eye. She clicked one after the other; the boats at the end of the horizon, the tall sea grasses and dunes along the shoreline, even the lobster trawler as it passed. No people.

Not her, not him nor the captain of the trawler, as he waved before hauling up out of the sea a line of lobster traps.

Tom had friends who returned from vacations with photos of far—away ports and historic buildings. No people, families or acquaintances they had met.

He never understood why. Thank God for his and Ivy's albums. He and Matt spent hours turning the pages, each picture with its own story, so that his son would know where he came from and how much his mother loved him. The ones Matt liked best were family holidays and playing with his mother and Aunt Rory on the beach.

Matt's favorite beach, Buzzard's Landing loomed ahead. Tom could make out the lopsided brambles and berry trees that lined the winding sandy paths. At the end of last summer, he took Matt on a whale—watching boat. They finished the day with a dune buggy ride, crossing the Landing and singing off key into the wind.

Kyra never focused the camera on him, or asked if he would snap her. Tom was surprised because she sounded family oriented.

Talking about brothers and parents, their life in North Carolina, hers now in Florida. He thought of her as a people person.

Maybe she didn't like him? That it was part of her job to play along with the police. That she didn't want a memento of their day on the water.

"Do you want to go further out?" he called out between tight lips.

"Actually, further in," her lilting voice gave him an easier feeling.

She had moved to the fisherman's chair on deck; plaited her red hair into two braids, pulled a white sun hat from her tote and put it on her head. Escaping tendrils framed her face. The braids whipping in the breeze

She rolled up her jeans. Slender feet disappeared into her boat shoes and she slipped off the bulky sweatshirt. Underneath, a blue cotton tee with spaghetti straps clung to her full breasts. Her bare shoulders had started turning light pink from the sun and he felt his heart pounding. He would love to run his fingers along her skin; so soft and smooth. He bet she felt tantalizingly warm.

It was becoming difficult controlling the desire rushing through him. How much longer could he go without a woman's body kneading into his? He had to contain himself, just imagine he was slipping her shirt off her shoulders and burying his face in her bare breasts. He exhaled a deep breath, transfixed by her movements.

Suddenly wanting a picture, a photo, and a remembrance for when she returned home and disappeared down south, he shouted, "How many photographs do you need of sea grasses and empty beaches?"

"Sometimes not all the shots come out."

"But you're using a digital? We.can see at once which photos are good." Maybe she needed changes of perspective or light. "Are you an artist?" he asked wondering, if she dabbled.

"No." Her half—chuckle floated in the air.

Then he got it. She was snapping the shoreline for her job. He didn't know whether to be amused, or annoyed. No wonder she didn't want to be followed and seemed so delighted when he took the wheel.

"When did you intend…" He stopped. Play it cool, Braden. See where this goes. The morning's tension had already dissipated. Why start all over again?

"What did you say?" She twisted to look at him. An inquiring smile lit up her face.

He grinned in return. He could play games too. Off in the distance, he could see the young couple's boat floating with the current in the opposite direction, their fishing lines dangling. The lone swimmer was gone. The tourist season, this time of year, was one of sight seeing and boating; and if you were lucky—whale watching. The ocean and the beaches were deserted, all theirs.

He turned the wheel, headed inward, might as well give her a closer view.

She clicked away, centering on the old Dickerson Estate and Buzzards Landing.

The sprawling house weather beaten with an improvised air that held so many memories for Barney as well as Rory. Even he held some with Ivy and Matt.

Did Kyra know about the trailer park? No one could build in the area without taking the RV site into consideration, especially, a company as huge as Harbors. This would split the town apart.

Those who wanted the park to disappear—versus—those who had called it home for so many years—and didn't want to leave. And what about RV visitors? They were a huge profit maker during the season. Returning year after year. A new RV park could show-up in a neighboring town with a monetary loss for Whales Bay.

Would Kyra wind up at the center of the turmoil? Maybe she would have to return from time to time.

A hollow feeling slipped through him. Was Megan's murder all about land acquisitions and luxurious accommodations?

Where did this put Kyra?

Had he let his emotions get the better of him? Had he ruled her out as a suspect before all the evidence had been collected?

A powerful boat rounded the bend parting the seas and bearing down on them.

"Tom," Kyra shouted, thrown sideways as the waves bounced them around.

In the oncoming boat, two men were hanging on to their seats and railing. The driver, long pale blond hair blowing in the wind, swiveled his head back and forth from Kyra and Tom to the wide-open ocean.

But no one laughed, no one waved, or brandished a bottle of beer, a fishing line, or shouted, "Sorry".

A cold dead fear grabbed his gut. Years of instinct took over. "Kyra, take the wheel—hurry!" He reached for his cell phone.

"What's going on?" She rushed—swaying—across the deck, anxiety written across her brow.

"Something isn't right. Grab the wheel!" He punched in a speed dial number, his eyes glued to the boat turning and heading in their direction. Closer and closer, it moved, the waves billowing until the boat pulled away, circled in a large arc, and then shot forward straight at them. Two men—definitely not dressed for fishing, or a day's cruise hustled about switching seats.

"What's happening?" Kyra swerved the wheel.

Tom shouted into the phone. "Twenty knots off Dickerson's Beach. Power boat, three men—they got guns."

Kyra clenched the wheel.

"Hunker down, they're within shooting range," he yelled, pushing the phone into its clip and pulling out his gun.

He barely heard the first shots. Just heard a zing as the first round buzzed past his ear. He rose halfway, returning fire. The shooters didn't expect it. Their boat weaved and darted.

"Stay down." Rising, he aimed again at the boat that zigzagged toward them.

"I'm heading in towards the inlet." Kyra turned the wheel hand over hand, didn't let up on the throttle.

For the second time, Tom didn't know if he got off a good shot. Then he saw two heads bobbing plus the driver. He had missed.

Kyra headed east. She appeared to be gaining speed. She swerved the wheel towards shore.

Tom yelled again into his cell for assistance.

Another bend and the Searay would be out of sight. But the killers wouldn't let up and kept pace closing the gap between the two boats.

Tom lifted his gun, and fired before they closed in. "I'll try keeping them at bay."

"This isn't an intruder," she shouted. "Or someone who wants my job."

"You are so right."

"How could this be happening on Cape Cod?"

One shooter was loading a gun; and Tom grabbed the opportunity, crouching along the side, to fire. The shooter went down, hard. It threw his partner off. The driver was shouting, looking every which way.

"Swerve Kyra, fast, head towards the next inlet. It's around the curve."

Kyra turned the wheel. "We're going too fast. I have to slow down."

Another spurt of gunfire from the second shooter and Tom yelled in pain.

"Are you hurt?"

"Just a graze."

The boat bumped, jostling them. "We hit something." She looked around. The shouting increased in tempo. A spray of bullets raked the port side making her cringe within.

"He pulled out another gun, more powerful." Tom aimed for the man at the helm.

"Our boat is hit," Kyra shouted.

"Stay down," Tom yelled. "I got the driver. The other shooter is scrambling for the wheel. Turn! Follow them. They're running."

"I can't. We're taking on water."

Then another spray of bullets splintered the wood below the railing and shattered the cabin windows. Kyra whirled around, and slipped. "Tom," she screamed, falling overboard into the water.

Tom ran to the side. Kyra was nowhere to be seen. In an instant, her head bobbed up—then went back under. Throwing down his gun he kicked off his loafers and jumped in swimming with all his strength to the spot where he saw her disappear.

She had to know how to swim, had to.

Maybe she was hurt, couldn't stay afloat. He had to find her. His heart beating so hard he thought it would burst.

This time he had a chance.

This time he could do something. Not like the day and the crash that killed Ivy. Then speeding to the accident scene, his heart pounding against his chest, there was nothing he could do to save her.

Now, he swiftly dove under the water praying that this time would be different. This time he could save Kyra.

CHAPTER ELEVEN

Kyra screamed, tried to grab onto the boat's railing as she went over, but missed. Her head hit the side followed by instant pain and total blackness.

The icy depths of the ocean woke her abruptly and an inner voice was shouting, "Kick. Kick."

Choking, she broke through the water and surfaced gasping for air, her chest throbbing. The high waves knocked her under once again. Only this time, as the water closed over her head she was able to hold her breath.

"Kick. Kick," her inner voice continued to scream while her legs barely moved.

"Kick. Kick." She heard the voice, pushed for the light, but couldn't reach it.

"Kick. Kick." Her lungs were about to burst. All she could do was flap her feet like the tail of a fish.

Suddenly, her legs stopped. Her body went limp and her eyes began to close.

Something grabbed her.

A strong, powerful arm circled her chest, pulling her upwards and breaking through the smothering water. Her head was lifted into the light of the day.

"Stay awake, Kyra. Don't leave me." She heard Tom's voice in her ear between deep gulps of air.

"Kick, kick," the inner voice shouted. "Help him. Help him. You can do it."

But her head felt like an explosion had gone off. Her forehead burned like raw meat; and everything was turning black as she bobbed in and out of the waves.

"Kick. Kick," seemed to echo all around her and the voice wouldn't go away. It was easier to let the strong arm and warm body propel her further into the light.

Gasping as both her mouth and nose took in the fresh sea air, she gagged.

"Kyra," Tom coughed. He couldn't stop, but didn't leave go. Clutching her with both arms, he treaded water, waiting for the spasm to end.

She clung to him in a haze, her head lolling onto his chest, but she couldn't respond. Trying to inhale, she slowly started moving her legs.

He lifted her higher out of the water. Rubbed her back. She started to heave, sputtered. Water dribbled from her mouth. He shifted about, smoothing the hair out of her eyes, "Kyra, talk to me."

She cringed when he touched her forehead and realized blood was running down her face. "I'm breathing," she choked. "I can see." She wrapped her arms round his neck. "Are they gone?" She panted, feeling as if her lungs would burst.

"Yes." He clutched her tight with one hand and using the other as a paddle parted the water.

Their wet clothes were pasted to their skin. She felt his powerful body as he enclosed her with his warmth and she felt safe and alive.

The sun disappeared behind the clouds. And the wind came up. Shivering, she pressed—tighter—entwined within him.

"Let's try for shore." With one arm holding her, he used a side—stroke with the other and headed inland to the beach.

But her muscles cramped. Her legs felt like lead weights were attached. There was no way she would make it. "I'll drag you down," she tried saying, but just a croak came out.

Blood dripped from his left arm. When he drew his hand across her face, she realized her blood was mixed with his. They seemed to be swimming in it, the water turning pink in their wake.

He patted her forehead. She still cringed from the pressure of his hand and the salt water that touched her wound. Pain radiated from her temple. Her head throbbed and she forced herself to exhale.

"Tom." But she couldn't continue. She tried to scream—leave—save your self.

Suddenly, a loud overhead motor zoomed above.

"It's the police helicopter," he shouted burrowing her head between his arm and his body. "And I can see the police boat."

Waves washed over them, anew.

"Stay where you are. We're picking you up," a loud speaker blared.

"We're not all bad. See, we do some good things." And he handed her up to waiting arms.

The next hour or so was a blur with police and medics swarming about the hanger. Rory arrived with bags of towels, jeans, sneakers and blankets.

Hot coffee and crackers miraculously appeared.

Barney showed up in Tom's car with enough hot Cape Cod chowder and home made bread for everyone milling about.

After EMT treated his arm and her forehead, everyone made an unanimous decision that neither one needed the hospital. Kyra promised to stop in for an x-ray and Tom bundled her into a blanket and drove her home. He pulled into the driveway about an hour and a half after they were lifted out of the water.

He scrambled for her keys and tossed her tote over his shoulder. Scooping her into his arms, he carried her inside and up the stairs. She had hooked her fingers in his belt and clenched it as if it was a loop on a life preserver.

"Easy, we're almost there."

"Don't leave me," she mumbled as he laid her down on the bed.

"A hot shower will do us both good." He raised himself.

"Hold me." She reached up held his face between her hands. Ran her fingers through his hair. "Don't leave me, please."

He wanted to devour her. Taste her, lick her, meld the two of them into one.

She wanted to be held.

He couldn't let go. Reached under her sweatshirt, pulled it over her head.

She wrapped her arms around his broad shoulders. He buried his face between her breasts unsnapping her jeans. She couldn't breathe, started panting.

"You're too tired. Banged up," he managed to say pulling away. "We should stop. Wait for a better time. I'll hold you while you sleep. And then we'll see."

"I don't want to sleep. Please. I need you, want you, now. Don't let me go. There is no better time." She started shivering. He lifted and carried her into the bathroom pressing her into his side with one hand while turning on the shower with the other.

Her shivering stopped and she lifted her face into the warm water, sighing. He spread his hands wide soaping and sliding across her body. Lifting her legs about him, he drove into her.

Exhausted, she lay curled around him. She felt warm and sated. "Can't move." She barely heard her own words.

"Don't." He put his finger across her lips, circled her belly with his other hand, and turned her so that she lay flat on the bed. Slowly, he licked his way down her legs and as she moaned he raised first one of her feet and then another placing each on one of his shoulders.

He nuzzled her toes, before licking his way back up each leg and dove into her core to the rhythm of her moans.

Her mind exploded in a rainbow of colors. She thought her heart and his were about to break through their chests. She felt his weight upon her body. And at this very moment, knew they were one.

⚜

The first rays of the morning sun started to light up the room. The aroma of coffee and eggs frying in the skillet made her realize how hungry she was.

She stretched languidly, not thinking or caring about anything. She looked about, mindless, and then it hit her.

Her close call. Her day and her night. And then her night of passion with Tom.

She bounced up. Breathed deep. She realized he must be making breakfast. They had ignored dinner. She grinned. He was too good to be true.

She swung her legs off the bed, but before her feet hit the floor, the phone started ringing in the silent bedroom. Her body tightened. Who would call so early? The sun was still rising out of the ocean. She made a grab for the receiver.

"Why did you shut your cell off?" JE demanded? "I had to fish around to find the house phone number."

"My cell is at the bottom of the ocean," her inner voice silently said. "Good morning. What's up?" Honey coated her words.

"I haven't heard a word about the property fronting the Sound or the trailer park nearby. Venture capitalists are walking in. We're serving cocktails. We're lunching, but no new information for me, The Chairman of the Board. Alesandro…."

"Forget Alesandro," she interrupted. I didn't want to inundate you with petty details. The Zoning Commissioner is on schedule. I'm meeting with the town's Mayor about the trailer park and personally paying a visit to the beachfront property."

All in good time, she thought. "AND, I'm on very good terms with Ms. Dickerson and her nephew!"

She made an instant decision not to mention that the Lieutenant and the Mayor were brothers-in—law.

CHAPTER TWELVE

*T*hree men! *Three men and they couldn't kill one woman. He slammed his cellphone down, shouted in the silence of his motel room, "What happened?"*

Shaking his fists into the air, he turned purple with another coughing spasm. He was still battling pneumonia from his nights spent offshore watching Ms. Stevens and her mansion. Had she seen him? Hired a bodyguard? He couldn't believe that. He was always so careful.

He also couldn't believe what he was just told. He pounded the table with a fist, shoved the chair out of his way; and raking his hand through his hair, stomped around the room, mumbling, "Who was the guy with her? With a gun?" His voice rose, "A gun?"

"God-Damn!" he shouted again and went into another fit of coughing.

One man dead, another injured and one on the run. He shook his head in disbelief. The shootout would be plastered all over the local papers as well as on the nightly news. And then the spin-doctors, he shuddered—imagined their talking heads hustling from one TV station to another.

He kicked the leather ottoman as he passed, paced back and forth between the windows and the small desk. He bit the inside of his mouth; and stopped dead in his tracks.

He had to call and find out what was really going on. But if he made the calls he couldn't demand answers. He felt like a fool; a word that was not normally used to describe him.

One dead, one injured, that God-damn woman alive and the police, if they haven't done so before, will now be poking their noses into everything.

Nothing gained. So much to lose.

And no nearer to his goal than when he arrived in Boston.

Maybe, maybe the next time, never mind maybe, he had to kill Ms. Stevens and soon. He certainly couldn't do worse than the three so-called hit men his employer recommended.

He rocked back on his heels, squinted in the direction of the door as if the three would—be killers had just entered and were standing in front of him. "You can kiss the fifteen thousand good—bye," he snarled.

What could they do if he didn't pay?

"Absolutely nothing."

Ms. Stevens was still out and about. Just one of the assailants left, a second half-maimed. If the Coast Guard became involved, he could make the FBI most wanted list.

If he wanted to continue in his field, this was not the notoriety he needed.

Yet, he took better precautions than the Harbors VP who never watched her back. According to what he was told, she operated on pure luck.

Maybe there was more to it than that. Maybe he was given erroneous information. Maybe Ms. Stevens wasn't a damn lucky bitch!

Maybe, she was dangerous as hell.

It didn't matter, either way, things were about to change.

CHAPTER THIRTEEN

After her early breakfast and a nap, Kyra awoke feeling as if she was enclosed in a cocoon of sensual delight. She stretched languidly. Smoothed her hand across the indents Tom had left on his pillowcase.

She wanted to relish the moment, relive her night with Tom. Not rush to dream or plan, or even anticipate the future.

For it could all blow up! Kyra rationalized live in the present and take what comes your way, at least, for now.

She turned her head, glanced at the clock and with a sudden rush moved from the bed into the shower. Lifting her face to the water, she moved her hand across her breasts. Still tender, they ached for his touch.

Kyra knew she was only postponing the inevitable. She had to calm her racing heart get back to reality, and her job. Today was her appointment with Andy McDermott. Her nervousness about the meeting returned, though Kyra would never admit it to anyone.

Deep inside, she wished she could ignore the business appointment her staff had made with the Whales Bay Zoning Commissioner.

She was definitely apprehensive about discussing properties, dollars and cents with the husband of the woman murdered in her boss' dining room.

But her job dictated otherwise. JE's six o'clock phone call had showed, he was still watching, demanding what he thought was his.

It wouldn't be long before James Enrico questioned why she hadn't met with Mr. McDermott. Being shot at while sailing off Whales Bay Beach would not be a satisfactory response. It would be best, if he didn't find out. Contending with Alesandro on the dunes didn't appeal to her.

Instead of lounging on the patio sipping a cup of coffee, Kyra dressed in a navy blue business suit, and drove into town.

Pulling into a visitor's spot under a large maple, she got out of her car and glanced around. About two blocks behind Town Hall, the office building that housed McDermott's law firm was standing on an expensive piece of property. Even the landscaping shouted big money. So did the entranceway.

Surprised, Kyra moved through the revolving doors into the black and grey marble lobby. Quite impressive!

A water fountain dominated the center and a small bank of elevators was on the right, a mirrored escalator to the left. Across from the front entrance, glass walls and doors overlooked a rear parking lot and beyond a maze of giant-high trees. She gave a slight shiver glad to be inside away from the March winds. Searching for McDermott's suite number on the computerized directory, she was surprised to learn that there were only three floors and three tenants. The building's ambience appeared rather sophisticated and expensive.

She'd expected numerous small suites with high rents to cover the building's expenses. Obviously, this didn't appear to be the case.

"Floor, please?" the British accented elevator voice asked.

"Third. Thank you." Wow. What an interesting feature. "Who put up the building?" Kyra asked aloud hoping the voice would answer.

Harbors Executive Towers had one that did.

In Manhattan, she and Alessandro held a conversation with the digital elevator voice all the way up to the twentieth floor. Maybe her research staff had made a second guffaw in underestimating the small Cape Cod town?

"Can't respond," the voice sounded perturbed. "Does not compute."

"Jeez!" Indeed, this was an expensive piece of equipment. Wait until James Enrico heard that Whales Bay wasn't so quaint, after all.

When Andy's secretary called to say he had to leave Town Hall mid-morning for his law firm, could Ms. Stevens meet him there? She had jumped at the chance to see McDermott on his own turf. Now, misgivings settled in.

"Third floor," the voice announced as the doors slid open with a whoosh.

"Goodbye," Kyra said and stepped out.

"Goodbye. Have a nice day," the voice responded sultrily. The doors whished closed.

She walked all the way to the end of the corridor, her navy and cognac colored shoulder strap bag bouncing against her hip, her red hair loose and curly. The only sound the click-clack of her demur heels on the marble tiled floor. She caught a glimpse of herself in the mirrored walls, smoothed the lapel on her fitted suit jacket and brushed stray tendrils over her bruised forehead. If the Zoning Commissioner hadn't heard about the shooting and her near drowning, why give him cause to see the bruises and bring up what happened? For all she knew, he could have arranged the attempt on her and Tom.

The very idea pushed bile up into her throat. She gulped swallowing it back down. What if she had been shot?

McDermott could argue that the same murderer was responsible for killing his wife. Ms. Stevens was always the intended victim, his wife an innocent bystander and he an innocent party.

Reaching the end of the hallway, Kyra stopped short in front of the etched, double glass doors, reached out to pull one open. Instead, both swung magically inward.

"Boy, more high tech," she murmured, entering the spacious black and white reception area.

"That we are, Ms. Stevens." The attractive brunette sitting at a rectangular smoky grey glass table beamed good-naturedly, and said, "Good Morning. Mr. McDermott will see you in five minutes. He's completing an international call. Please take a seat. Can I get you coffee, tea, something cold?"

"Some water." Kyra needed to wash away the bitterness in her throat."

"I'm sorry Mr. McDermott's secretary, Ms. Sawyer isn't here to greet you, but she was detained at the Council meeting." The receptionist placed a Waterford glass and linen napkin on the small table beside Kyra's chair.

"Thank you," Kyra said, thinking her staff definitely had to do additional research on Whales Bay with emphasis on Andy McDermott's operations. She drank the water, replaced the glass on the table and looked around.

It appeared that the inner walls were glass so wherever she stood or sat Kyra could see straight out to the ocean and the horizon.

She wondered if McDermott was an owner, or a partner in the building? This entire operation didn't cost chicken—feed. Could he afford the taxes and upkeep all by himself?

"Mr. McDermott is free, now." The receptionist pressed a button on a small panel near her computer and a pair of twin doors to the right slid open.

A broad shouldered man wearing a navy blue, single breasted Armani suit was walking around a one hundred gallon tank feeding tropical fish. His polka dotted silver tie matched his shirt. He had brown hair styled and sprayed to the side, the back ending at his shirt collar. His eyes so vivid blue, Kyra was positive he wore contacts. He looked about ten years older than Megan.

"I'm sorry for your loss," she said, as she approached, hand outstretched. "I had no idea Miss Polk was your wife when my assistant made the appointment."

Sheer surprise covered his face. He looked dumb struck. She swore his jaw dropped and a pasty color replaced the quick glimpse she had when entering, of a robust complexion.

"Did anyone mention...?" McDermott's voice trailed off as they shook hands. Quickly regaining his composure, he motioned to a visitor's chair facing his executive desk. "Please."

She noticed he favored his left side as he put the can of fish food in the built-in credenza and sat down.

"Megan was well known in real estates circles," he said. "But, using her maiden name gave her a certain freedom. She claimed married to a town's Zoning Commissioner had its drawbacks." He smirked as if to say isn't that ridiculous. Lacing his fingers together, he rested them on his chest. His eyes stayed glued to her face, and he asked in a hoarse voice, "Has anyone told you how much you resemble Megan?"

"No. But I saw it."

"McDermott propped a hand under his chin rubbed a couple of fingers across his lower lip, seemingly mesmerized by the sight of her. "And this was when?"

"When?" He knew damn well, she thought. "When I discovered her body." She almost choked on the last word, but held his gaze.

Shadows of sunlight streaked through the windows lighting the well—appointed black and white office. She found herself tilting her head not to blink. He had to realize how uncomfortable she was with the morning sun shining into her eyes, but he made no attempt to walk over and draw the blinds.

At that moment, she was positive he automatically did it for certain visitors. Otherwise, he used it as a tool for maintaining control.

But she had no intentions of playing his game. She nodded at the bank of windows. "Do you mind?"

He got up and tilted the white wood verticals.

"Oh, I'm so sorry," he said turning while watching the shadows cross the room.

A cold chill crept up her spine. She forced herself out of the chair and walked to a white carved and marble table. "I didn't realize you had your own law practice."

Surprise registered over his face as he saw her examining the framed law degree, incorporation papers and graduation snapshots artfully displayed around an ornate crystal bowl of red silk roses.

He stood immobilized, anger etched around his mouth, waited for her to return to her chair before he sat down. He seemed jarred by her movements to roam around his office. She knew not why and certainly didn't care.

He started talking as soon as she crossed her legs. "My firm used to be much larger, but since becoming zoning commissioner, I had to turn away a good many clients. Conflict of interest, you know." His tone implied he understood where she was coming from and that he'd been asked and had answered such questions many times throughout the years.

She was always amazed at how many friends elected officials could garnish. Probably enough to make up for all the cases they had to relinquish. The right friends in the right places could embellish a career and lifestyle. It was then that she decided she really didn't like him.

She couldn't say why. Whether it was his tone or his mannerisms, or what Tom had told her, but eventually, she would pin it down. Murderous! Arrogant! Perhaps a fifty—fifty split.

Then again to be fair, she was a person of interest in his wife's death. This might have affected his attitude towards her. But she knew it hadn't affected hers to his. If anything, she should have been sympathetic. Actually, the man annoyed her.

"What does a JEC executive want in our little town?" he asked.

"Not much." She smiled. "It's more like a busman's holiday. Comparing the beach style here to mine in Miami."

He burst out laughing. "For one, Miami is very sophisticated. On the Cape, we're rural, almost quaint."

"Not in this building," she chuckled. "I'm quite impressed."

He nodded his head, both his eyebrows quirked and he smiled with a grimace of appreciation. "Thank you."

Enough small talk, she thought, best to get to the reason why her office made the appointment. "My company was curious about your town's zoning ordinances. Do they allow commercial buildings higher than three floors?"

"So far not in Whales Bay, though several other Cape Cod localities go as high as four or five, and then some."

He smirked. "I know Harbors likes them taller. Was that why you and Megan were meeting? Doing groundwork on that problem? If so, you should have included me. Variances are possible if the Zoning Commissioner is modern and interested in development."

Every muscle in her body tightened. Stay cool. He's got his hand out—but! Don't let him see he caught you unaware. "I think there is a misunderstanding. I never met with your wife, or had planned too."

"Megan was quite explicit," McDermott said in a chilled tone.

"As you can see from today, I start my negotiations with the person in charge." Her thoughts raced like a ticket tape around her mind. Megan wasn't feeding you information. She already reported you to the police for brutality. She was out to get even. Did you kill her to stop her accusations and tarnish your reputation?

"I'm positive you're mistaken," Kyra said hearing the steel in her voice. She uncrossed her legs, about to stand, remembered her position as Vice President of a national corporation and what would be her next move. "If you have a list of the nearby towns and their building variances, it would be greatly appreciated and we could then discuss what the next step will be."

"And then?"

"And then we could have lunch and analyze some of the possibilities."

She stood offered her hand, and smiled. "By the way, I'm having a small cocktail party next week. I know it's quite soon after Megan's death, but I would like you to attend. Bring any guests you care too. Several people you know will be there."

"Who?"

"Local people, of course, like Mayor Dickinson and Chief of Police Williams. But several people we're both acquainted with from Boston are driving down. Lawrence Ellridge for one." She held her breath.

"Ellridge!" His voice rose slightly, then he exhaled and locked eyes with her from across the desk. "Not familiar."

Says who? She had caught the flicker of fear in his eyes.

CHAPTER FOURTEEN

Kyra pressed the elevator DOWN button. Taking a steadying breath, she watched the bouncing ball. Felt like she needed a hot shower to wash away the effects of dealing with Andy McDermott.

The door whooshed open. She stepped in, oblivious to the building's décor on her way down.

At JEC Industries, she negotiated and played so many games of strategy that she knew when an opposing party was being evasive and wanted something that was not placed on the table.

She was also stunned when McDermott used his dead wife to emphasize his position as Zoning Commissioner. He had either lied in his silk suit and polished office, or knew Megan did before she was murdered.

It seemed as though Megan had taunted Andy about her ability to pull off a major deal without him and the situation got carried away between husband and wife.

Or did Megan unknowingly meet with Kyra's impersonator who had already telephoned Victoria Dickenson?

For a moment, Kyra wondered was she wrong to assume the same woman used her name a second time and was participating in some sort of telephone scam.

Absolutely not!

Two women were too much of a coincidence. She couldn't believe that one woman would even do such a brazen thing.

Of course, there was the possibility that Megan tried to arrange her own appointment with the VP from JEC Industries; and that was the reason she was at James Enrico's summer mansion.

Megan had tracked Kyra down, knew her destination and was waiting for her.

But the murderer arrived, saw a redheaded woman and thinking she was Kyra—killed her.

If so, then Tom was right.

She was the intended victim, but what was the scam?

And who wanted her dead?

Tom had asked for a list.

A List!

Kyra couldn't imagine a list.

Shuddering, she leaned against the elevator wall. It wasn't her place to find the answers. That was Tom's job. He was the prime detective on the case. The one game she never played was Victim. And she had no intentions of starting now.

It was up to her to clear her head and continue to do what she did best. Concentrate on her priorities and her position on the Board of Directors. Kyra understood there were people who would die for her job, and people who would kill for her job. So, maybe she would be wise to watch every move she made.

Was it possible Tom was right?

Realizing two days had passed since she initiated a phone call to James Enrico was something she had to be careful about, as well as their communicating. It was her place to periodically call him, not only be responsive to his messages.

This was the first project she hadn't touched base with him on a daily basis. The murder investigation was keeping her off point, as was the man who headed it.

Perhaps JE would think she was locked up in meetings, or guessed she had taken out a boat and was exhausted from her day on the water. No one, not even the Chairman of the Board, would imagine she had become a killer's target as she sailed along the Cape Cod coastline.

Actually, she had fueled his anger this morning by not calling. There were no excuses. She knew better.

It was easier to close her eyes remembering when she lay with Tom as the sun slowly sank into the sea and the moon took its place high above.

After Tom left in the early hours of the new day she hungered for him. Her skin burned down to her toes. She could feel his mouth nuzzling every inch of her body and his tongue flicking the nipples on her breasts. She couldn't remember feeling this way before with any other man.

Wetness lined her panties. She slumped against the wall. And jumped, startled, as the digital voice announced, "The Lobby."

She blinked. The elevator stopped. The door whooshed open. Kyra couldn't move. "Have a good day," the voice titillated.

Camera! Boat! Those were on top of her to-do list, and tonight, dinner—quid pro quo. She could satisfy herself and satisfy James Enrico with new information.

She strutted into the lobby. So far, she was working the situation. Her so-called fling was under control, as well as her encounter with the Whales Bay Zoning Commissioner.

Which reminded her. She stopped in front of the computerized directory. An accounting firm had offices on the second floor and a real estate firm on the first. Their suite of rooms was tucked on the other side of the escalator.

Was it the same firm where Megan had worked? Walking to the far side of the building, Kyra glanced through the company's double glass doors.

Several people were on the phone while simultaneously surfing their computers. A sleek fortyish woman stood in a doorway talking to a man behind a desk. No one looked familiar. No one appeared hassled. She watched for a moment, debated whether her presence would stir things up and decided to leave. She'd wait until she had more information before barging in.

Hurrying through the revolving doors, Kyra took a deep breath. The fresh air felt great. All of a sudden, the building seemed storm—angry, claustrophobic and unclean.

Clicking her car doors open, she threw her purse on the passenger seat, turned the key and moved into traffic. Without one solid piece of evidence, she now thought that the showy, expensive building didn't belong in Whales Bay after all. It represented a center for doing business that was not on the up—and—up.

Slowly, she headed down Main Street searching for an electronic store. There had to be one, to lure the tourists in and help town residents who couldn't drive to Malls for every emergency.

Sure enough, she spotted one across from the diner.

Inside, they had her exact digital camera and smart phone that went overboard during the shooting.

Feeling connected to the world once again, Kyra sighed in relief as she returned to her car. She felt the sun beaming down on her every step. A few clouds fluffy like giant cotton balls were heading out to sea and she had the overwhelming desire to take a blanket and lounge on the beach.

But suddenly, Vince's face flashed before her, and she gasped. There was no way he would rent another boat to the primary suspect in Megan's murder especially now, after she destroyed and sank his Sea Ray. Her hands clenched the steering wheel.

Tom had said he would take care of the paperwork.

Never said he would help rent a second boat? But she had to get back on the water and take the promised snapshots for JE. Even though she realized it could interfere with Tom's job, she hoped he would know what to do. But how far would he go?

She was also mindful of JE. Though doubtful, if the shoot—out had made it to the Florida newspapers, she recalled his words. "The Social Media was another story." She also had to act on her promise to photograph the beachfront property the company must have for their proposed resort.

Her back—up phone that she fished out of her lingerie drawer this morning vibrated against her waist. She didn't recognize the number, knew it had to be someone she met on the Cape.

She pressed TALK.

"How are you doing?" Tom's voice sent a shiver of delight through her body.

"Fine," she said smiling from ear to ear.

"Where are you?"

"On Main Street getting into my car."

"So close? Can you drop in?"

"I…" She hesitated. "Is it important?"

"I would like you to look over my report about what happened yesterday."

"Do you need my input?" She cringed. Was he going to play questions and answers? Put her on the spot and ask once again for the list of who wanted her dead?

"More like some observations. I need a signed statement from you. As well as information for the insurance papers."

She swallowed hard understanding he had his responsibilities. She had forgotten all about hers this morning walking around like a teen-ager floating on a cloud and daydreaming. "I'm on my way."

Tom watched Kyra settle into his visitor's chair. She took the computer printout he handed her and began reading without so much of a kiss on his cheek, or a hug.

Was he thinking inappropriately? What with glass walls and doors, he was thinking like a kid just coming of age. Kyra appeared to have more sense.

Her very essence—the tilt of her head, a wayward curl, the motion of her foot as she crossed her legs—turned him on. After last night, all he wanted was to close the blinds and tear her clothes off.

Kyra, on the other hand, appeared polite and professional, as if nothing had happened between them? Maybe he had her all wrong. Maybe she was just mature and polished. A person of the moment—like she said after their first kiss—flitting from one experience to another and could care less about what he thought or desired. A businesswoman on the move invested only in her job.

He sat quietly, drinking her in, waiting for comments, hoping to see a sign of affection, even a wink, and wondered.

Was last night a thank you gift for saving her life? He knew how she felt about short-term relationships, which he favored and she distrusted. At times, she had talked about her feelings, as they had grown more intimate.

He'd never mixed his personal and professional lives before. He needed to get a grip. He had a case to solve. Too much was at stake. He could not evade what she called his game of questions and answers. He sat, watching and waiting. His thumb moved back and forth along his jawline.

She finished reading the report, looked up. "It's concise. I don't know what you want me to add?"

"Did I leave anything out?"

"It's fine."

"Did any of the men in the other boat look familiar?"

"No."

"Shout something I didn't hear."

"Not that I can think of." Annoyance seeped into her tone formed creases in the corners of her mouth.

He swept his eyes over her. Felt a loss for words. "You were there. Shot at. Aren't you angry? Doesn't one thing stand out more than all the others?"

"Of course! You saved me. But the men were strangers, perhaps, a couple of guys who drank too much and thought a cop and a woman made good targets."

"We don't believe they were from the area."

"Is there any sign of them? They didn't evaporate into thin air."

"They pulled ashore further up the coast and it appears that they sank the boat. The Coast Guard is searching the waters."

"They disappeared?" she asked dumb struck.

"Yes."

"All three?"

"We found tire tracks, footprints, blood. More than likely, a fourth man parked and waited until they returned."

"But you thought you hit two. Didn't either one check into a local hospital or go to a nearby doctor?"

"So far, no," he hesitated. "I think I killed one, or wounded him badly. He fell and I didn't see him get up. The Coast Guard is looking for a body. The other men could have left him in the boat or thrown him overboard." He sat straight up, touched her arm.

"Who knew you were renting a boat, or going out to snap photos?"

She bit down on her lower lip. "I…I told a few people in my Florida office before I left, but never mentioned exactly when I would. It was a spur of the moment decision to go yesterday."

"Did you tell anyone in Boston?"

"No. Until I arrived on the Cape, I never was in or knowingly met someone from this area. And no one I know walks around with a gun, or fires it, except you."

She closed her eyes, fought the urge to burst into tears. "I'm sorry. But I am so upset. Since I arrived, it's one frightening incident after another. And you're always playing detective. One question after another."

"Kyra, I don't mean to hassle you, but Whales Bay hasn't seen a homicide in almost ten years. Now, we're investigating a brutal murder that occurred upon your arrival, plus two attempts on your life. And I thought," he paused.

"What?"

"That after the shooting yesterday, you would feel, or realize you were connected to Megan's murder."

"I thought about it. Those men were shooting at me, too. But I still don't have a clue to who would want to kill me."

"And that's my reason for asking questions. Sometimes they remind people of something in the past that could be a link."

"I can't imagine who would be so angry and vindictive at me."

She turned her head, eyes roving towards the hallway as if wanting to escape. Shrugging, she stood, played with her shoulder strap. "Sorry Tom, I don't know how I can be of more help. And I have... a new problem. Something ...that affects my job."

"What?" His eyes narrowed. A tightness gripped his mouth.

"I have to rent another boat?"

"You're kidding?" He clenched the arms of his chair. "More important than your life?" Pushing himself up, he moved quickly around the desk, blocking her path.

"I must take pictures of the shoreline and e-mail them to my boss. It is imperative. But I don't know where and who will rent me another boat..." her voice trailed off.

"Easy," he interjected, tilted her chin up and locked his eyes with hers. "Let me think about it. Don't do anything rash until I call. Promise?"

She nodded, touched her lips gently to his, and patted the oversized band aide on his arm. "I'm sorry. I feel it's my fault, but I didn't plan what happened."

His heart jumped a beat.

She walked out of the office and into the hallway, realized she hadn't invited him over.

"Ms. Stevens, can we talk for a moment," Chief Williams' voice stopped her cold. A tall, thin man was standing with the Chief on his threshold. He glanced quickly at her and then headed in the opposite direction. Williams braced the door open with one hand waited for her to enter.

What did he want now? She gritted her teeth.

"How are you? You look none the worse after your near drowning. We tried to phone late yesterday afternoon, but you didn't answer."

The door shut behind her.

He flourished a hand toward a visitor's chair. "Please, sit down."

His shirt was stiff as gunmetal. The ribbons and medals across his chest gleamed in the rays of sun streaming through the open slats of the window blinds. He sat across the corner of his desk and pushed a miniature slot machine filled with jellybeans in her direction.

"Try some. A birthday present from my wife."

"No, thank you." She smiled and sat back.

"We were waiting for you to come in."

"Why?"

Ignoring her question, he asked, "We were anxious to know if you knew any of the men in the boat?"

"Absolutely not!" Her insides twisted into a knot and she sat forward.

"Not even a scorned boyfriend, or a disgruntled ex-JEC employee?"

"No." She pursed her lips felt her cheeks burn, but couldn't stop her glare.

"Perhaps, someone who knew you were going to rent a boat for the day?"

"No one. And I already answered the same questions for Lieutenant Braden."

"I wanted to hear it from your lips." He leaned toward her and gave a wide grin.

She inhaled and swallowed. Wanted to kick him in the shins and leave, but thought better of it. "Then, I think you should ask him yourself and this way you could check up if I'm telling the truth. Between your men and the Lieutenant's there are several cops patrolling my house. So, I guess you know my itinerary for yesterday morning." She made a motion to rise.

"I'm not finished." Williams half turned, opened a manila folder and skimmed through the pages. "The first interview after Megan died, did not mention where you stopped for gas on the way down to the Cape. Timing is very important in proving your innocence or guilt."

"I didn't."

"Didn't what?"

"Stop for gas. I rented a car at Logan and it was filled to the top. So there was no need too. Anything else?"

"We could do this the easy way, Ms. Stevens, or the hard way. JEC Industries can't enclose you in a protective shield all the time. I was notified that you were involved in another murder in Florida. Is that true?"

She stared blankly across at him. Felt her nerves tighten and her mind whirling like a top. "Are you politely accusing me of being a serial killer?"

The phone rang. He reached behind him and picked up, his eyes not moving from her face.

"Williams!" His expression changed and he stood, brows arched, he walked around his desk. "Hold on." He covered the receiver with his hand and the words snapped out of his mouth. "That's all for now, Ms. Stevens. Our interview will have to continue another time. Just don't leave town." His icy glare shot darts at her. She felt his eyes bore into her back and follow her down the hall.

She glanced quickly over her shoulder as she turned the corner. The Chief's eyes were riveted to her every move. He still hadn't returned to his phone.

How did he learn about Isabella's murder? And did he tell Tom?

What would make him interface with the Miami police?

Tom hadn't alluded to it. But did that mean anything? The two men didn't get along. Professional jealousy permeated their relationship, but they still could be working together. Perhaps Williams had looked beyond his scope for an angle that could prove her guilty.

She felt as if someone had left her dangling in the wind.

CHAPTER FIFTEEN

Kyra unpacked the groceries and then began programming her new phone and camera. She was just about finished when Tom called.

"Great news. Barney loaned me his boat for tomorrow morning. I have an early appointment at my Hyannis Port office, but I'll be back by nine. Could you meet me at his marina?"

"Of course. Thank you so much, Tom. Are you going with me?"

"You don't think I would let you go out alone? Do you?"

"I hoped not." She chuckled. "And if you want to come by later for a quid-pro dinner...?" Her voice trailed off.

"I..." he hesitated. "I have to stop off at the Whales Bay Police Station late afternoon, and I promised Matt we would eat together and spend some time.

"Have a good evening, and say hello to Matt for me."

"I will." His deep voice filled her with a sense of warmth and affection. But most of all Tom understood how important photographing the shoreline meant to her and she appreciated his thoughtfulness.

Though she was trying to separate her private from her professional life, he had stepped in to help bridge the gap.

That night, she worked till almost eleven on her computer, completed several reports and requests for additional information from her staff. She stored everything in a new computer file and sent an e-mail to JE, still omitting any mention of the shootout on Nantucket Sound. By the time she finished, Kyra was ready for bed.

Putting the laptop into the large executive desk and locking the drawer, she turned the library lights off, flicked the hall lights on. She stopped in the kitchen for a snack, and balancing a half glass of milk and a miniature pastry, decided to enjoy them in bed watching TV. But before she could walk out of the kitchen, she stopped short.

The rear gate was swinging softly in the night breeze. She hadn't heard it earlier and was positive she locked the gate after watching the sunset from the beach. Hesitating a moment or two, she put the glass and dessert plate on the table.

Should she call Tom?

Should she call the police?

Maybe the wind had picked up?

"Nerves?" she exclaimed aloud. "That's all it is."

But before she could take another step, someone jiggled the rear doorknob that led from the garden.

Kyra grabbed the largest knife from its rack on the counter. A loud noise seared through her. Not knowing what it was, she rushed to the side of the window, and tried peeking around the corner of the Cape Cod curtains.

"Nothing," she murmured to herself, watching. The starry sky above blinked down on the deserted lawn and she heard the swell of waves washing up on the sand. The glow from the sky reflected on the rolling water. How could anything so beautiful be so frightening?

A loud bang slammed against the outer door. Was it a tree branch, or was someone trying to force the door open?

Instantaneously, she remembered, what Officer Pirro had explained and she ran to the panel of switches and buttons alongside the kitchen wall phone.

She flicked the large green switch and all the outside overhead lights lit up the house and grounds.

The estate must look like a sunny day at noon, she thought, as lights flooded the kitchen and hallway seeping in at the corners of blinds and curtains throughout the building.

By the time, she returned to the window, somebody was sprinting over the back lawn, jumped over the gate and was running along the beach disappearing from view into the blackness of an ocean-side March night. She barely made out long legs, white sneakers, jeans and a dark hoodie.

She dragged the mudroom's utility table over to the door and braced it under the knob. Pulling several oversized pots and pans out of the closets, she scattered them across the floor and into the foyer all the way up to the top of the stairs.

Leaving the bedroom TV on, she fell asleep agonizing over who was stalking her? It couldn't be Gregg. No matter what Tom thought, Gregg was in Florida and according to the Miami papers devoting his time to a new Museum exhibit.

Should she check?

Her fingers closed around the knife handle protruding from under the adjoining pillow on the empty side of the bed.

＝‹‡ ‡›＝

"Good morning," Kyra called as she walked along the ramp to the dock. "What a glorious day." She drank in the sky and the sea and the soft spring breezes. And Tom.

He looked like an action hero as he moved around the boat putting things in order. A Band-Aid still covered the graze on his arm from the wayward bullet. A blue tee shirt outlined his broad shoulders and upper arms. He wore swim shorts and white deck shoes and as usual took her breath away.

"Hi, how're you doing?" Giving her a large grin, he crossed to the side, pulling the brim of his Cape Cod tourist cap up over his forehead. He reached for her hand and with his other, circled her waist lifting her over the railing.

She laughed with pleasure.

He leaned over for a kiss drawing her lower lip between his own at the same time holding her tight against his chest. She could see his worried eyes studying her face.

"What?" She cringed within. Please, don't let him spoil the day by playing questions and answers.

"Did anything happen last night?" He murmured holding her upper arms, kneading them gently with his thumbs. They moved round and round, in little circles.

An ache pressed below her belly.

She swallowed hard, shook her head no. "Why?"

"Your place was lit up like Christmas decorations. Everyone in town thought you were having a party and that they weren't invited."

"No one rang the bell, or complained."

"Officer Pirro drove by, saw that your bedroom TV was on, so he thought you pressed the wrong switch on the kitchen panel."

"He was right."

"So, everything was fine."

"Absolutely!"

"But if it wasn't, you would have called me?"

"Of course." She pulled away.

He let go.

She walked down to the galley and put her things in a small cabinet. Reached into her tote, searched for her camera, and then covered her eyes with sunglasses. Hearing someone running along the dock she glanced up through the transom.

"Hay, Tommy, wait?" Barney jumped aboard taking deep breaths. "I got a cap for Kyra, too." His voice echoed down into the cabin. He was holding a matching blue cap like Tom's.

She slid the camera's wristlet over her hand and turned to go.

"What happened Barney?" Tom's voice struck a nerve in her body.

She stood motionless. The two men seemed to read each other without a sound. She felt awkward, but couldn't move.

"McDermott just phoned. His office was broken into last night. His secretary reported it when she arrived this morning."

"Anything taken?"

"A couple of files and some personal papers."

"And?" Kyra saw Tom tilt his head, lock eyes with his brother—in—law.

"Some Whales Bay officers went by, but Andy is not only angry, he's frightened. Feels this has something to do with Megan's murder. He hoped you would look into it."

"I should. I will, but...not this moment. Did he talk to Williams?"

"The Chief's name didn't come up. Andy called me at the restaurant because he wants you to personally investigate. He didn't want to phone the station. He believes if he asked for you, the local cops would object."

"Tell him, I'll be by this afternoon. That I'm working on another case and can't come over now."

Barney's brows arched in question. "Isn't it all the same case?" His voice rose.

"Connected, but not the same. Yesterday, was two attempted murders and the victims were lucky."

"So, why go out again?" Barney demanded. "You got a kid and people who love you. You're more important than a bunch of pictures and someone's job."

The words went through Kyra like a sharpened stiletto. She heard herself gasp. Wanted to run home and crawl into bed hide under the covers. And realized there was more to this than Megan's murder and the intruder who consistently was out to get her.

She had to be patient, calm herself down. She had asked and Tom had delivered. Was it wrong of her to accept the boat even if it was just for the morning and a quick cruise up the shoreline?

"Easy, it'll be all right," Tom said. He locked eyes with Barney. "If it makes you feel any better, call Andy. Tell him I will stop off this afternoon. I can't leave what I'm doing now."

Barney shook his head. "We're talking about two different things." Muttering something under his breath, he jumped onto the dock.

"Barney doesn't want you to go because of yesterday's shooting," Kyra said walking up the stairs, her voice rising with each step. "He's worried. I'm worried. What would happen to Matt, if something happens to you?"

"Rory and Barney were always my back-up. Even in New York! I've made my decision. Don't worry about it. I've never been frightened by a case, or off a case."

"Tom, you can leave if you want too. I can handle the boat, myself. No one is going to attempt another assignation, so soon."

Though he had the more dangerous job, she realized at this time, that she was the one bringing the most danger to their relationship.

"I will not let you go out alone after what happened, yesterday." He leaned into her and smiled. "Anyway, I was looking forward to just you and me and a peaceful spring day." He kissed the tip of her nose. "Pull the anchor up and I'll start the motor. Let's try and not worry about anything."

"Aye, aye Captain." She made a quick salute with her hand, breathed in deep. All of a sudden, she felt positively giddy.

Tom hustled to the controls and she heard the motor rev.

He hadn't left her to fend for herself even if it had something to do with her job.

They got back a little after noon. A tall young man sprinted across the dock and helped them tie up to the Cleats. Tom gave Kyra a quick kiss promised to see her that evening and headed for the parking lot.

Kyra stopped in the restaurant looking for Barney to finalize her order for the party, but he was out. She left a deposit and a thank you note for lending her his boat. She really wanted to approach him about his aunt's property, but had to put her thoughts on the back burner.

Perhaps after the party.

She had to separate her job from her personal life.

Making her way to the local liquor and wine store, Kyra went over the soft and hard drinks with the owner's wife.

Jean, a thin blond lady offered some crackers with a dip. "Taste one. Please. I make the dip myself. Some of the Boston City people place orders during the year and I ship the dip to their homes up north."

"It's great," Kyra said chewing slowly. The sea air had made her hungry and she was starved. The dip was delicious and she ate several nodding with approval.

"I know we missed catering the party you had last night, but I hope that after next week's event you'll think of us again. Mr. Cassel used us all the time when he was in town."

"I didn't have a party yesterday. Actually, next week is the first one since I arrived." She recalled Tom's remark about the lights and realized now why he was perturbed.

"Oh! So why was your place lit up?" Jean asked.

"I pressed the wrong button," Kyra said in a self- depreciating tone.

"Then why didn't you shut the lights off?"

I was afraid, she thought, but instead said with a feeble smile, "I fell asleep watching TV." Shrugging, she ordered several pounds of the dip and took a container home for cocktails with Tom. She stood, thanking Jean and imagined the new story that would go around town by tomorrow.

A little later, Kyra turned off the main road, and went down the narrow country lane leading to the Cassel mansion. Mrs. Nelson was dusting the downstairs when she arrived.

"Well, everything looks fine. I'll arrive early Sunday morning to set things up. I have a part-time college student, Alex who helps with large parties. Did you ask Jean to arrange for the bartenders?."

"Yes."

"Great. I thought there would be a mess after last night's event, but you did a pretty good job by yourself."

Startled, Kyra let out a chuckle. "Didn't have a party yesterday. Would have called you, if I did. But thanks for thinking about me. I will be sure to tell Mr. Cassel what a great job you are doing."

"Do you need anything for dinner? Any guests?

"No, thanks."

"Everyone in town was talking about yesterday's event. Even my friends, but I insisted you didn't have one."

"And you were so right," Kyra sighed turning away, as she thought. I was frightened to death and afraid of the people who keep trying to break in. The words went round and round in her head like a ticker tape.

She put her purchases in the fridge, took the sandwich Barney had left for her lunch and grabbed a cold beer. With her camera, she went into the library and sank into the high back leather chair facing the desk.

Closing her eyes, she tried thinking about nothing. Not of men, or the sea, or her job. She just sat enjoying her lunch until the vacuum started. Mrs. Nelson was probably cleaning the minuet crumbs from last night's uninvited guests.

She had forgotten how small town life functioned? Wondered what information she could pick up on the sly about the makers and shakers of Whales Bay. She might even be able to strike a coo. To her astonishment though, there was more talk of her so—called party than the shooting attack on her and Tom.

Swiveling around to the computer, she took the SD card out of the camera and put it into the SD slot in the laptop. She had shot at least four dozen photographs and could not send so many by e-mail. Instead, she uploaded the photos to Cloud Storage on the Internet in order for JE to review them. This would also make an excellent backup.

She finished by sending JE an e-mail with instructions on how to retrieve the shoreline photos.

Another obstacle was out of the way. Now, all she had to do was prepare her quid-pro dinner and share the new murder information with James Enrico that she would glean from Tom. Her boss would be content for another week or two.

And by then, she would have plenty of party gossip.

CHAPTER SIXTEEN

Tom propped his fork and knife on the plate and leaned back in the chair. He had taken off his tie and unbuttoned the collar when he arrived. He looked weary. Kyra couldn't even imagine the day he must have had.

"Did you see Andy McDermott?" she asked.

"Ah, yes, I forgot this is a quid-pro dinner."

The remark bothered her, but choosing to ignore it, she nodded at his dinner plate. "Did you like?"

"Delicious. What kind of fish?"

"Haddock from Barney's. I topped it with a Meniere sauce." She felt like they were reciting lines from a food channel program and almost laughed out loud.

"How many calories?"

"Absolutely none." She crossed her fingers in front of her face and he smiled with her.

"Then I don't have to feel guilty about enjoying it."

"Definitely not, and wait till you taste my calorie—free—sugar—free cheese cake."

A quick smile and he rolled his eyes. "Can't wait. I hope my information lives up to expectations and worthy of your dinner." The amusement disappeared. His voice hardened.

"Tom, if you have difficulty talking about different aspects of the case, it's okay with me."

"But will it be okay with Mr. Cassel?"

"I never said I was sharing the info with him."

Tom tilted his head gave a wry grin. "You didn't have too. I knew. But I'm glad that it's out and in the open. As the prime investigator, I have to be careful with any information I release. There are things I might say to Kyra Stevens that I cannot say to the Vice President of JEC Industries. I trust you will use your best judgment and when necessary, hold back on what you tell Mr. Cassel. I'm walking on thin ice with this one, Kyra."

He swore the color drained from her face. Realizing he sounded as if he had made an accusation, or thought about cutting off the relationship because of it, he stopped speaking. Reached across the table for her hand.

What he'd really wanted to say was not only the sex great, but he wanted to be with her—admired her—her quickness—her cleverness. If only she would stop coming up with motive and opportunity every time something happened in Whales Bay. Either she was guilty as hell, or someone was definitely out to get her.

Maybe his gut was right. End the affair, before the case ended his career.

Yet, at this moment, he couldn't say such a thing. For she was inching her way into his soul and he couldn't deny his attraction to her. Wished she would confide in him. Trust him. "Kyra, I care for you." He stopped. For where could this relationship go, anyway? They lived more than sixteen hundred miles apart. Each had a demanding career.

Besides he was the one who always wanted a short, sweet affair! Didn't think he could handle a second deep and loving marriage that might end in a loss. While according to Kyra, her needs were just the opposite of his.

He intertwined his fingers with hers. "Sometimes I feel…"

"I have feelings for you too, Tom," she interjected as if she preferred not hearing about his. "And, I'm not using you. I didn't murder anyone. I only tell JE what I have too. It's part of my job. I would never knowingly do, or say anything that would hurt you. Maybe we became too close too soon."

She felt her eyes fill with tears, took a deep breath and stared into the space over his shoulder. "I become frightened at times," her voice sounded hollow. "Alone in this barn of a house. I know it isn't nerves. I've lived by myself for years. I…I feel that I'm being stalked. I know something similar happened in Florida. But this is different. I don't know whom or why. If I did, I would tell you."

"Did something happen that I don't know about? And how many times?"

She bit down on her lower lip, shrugged. "There are nights I hear a small boat off shore. Other times noises—whispers of someone prowling outside the house and grounds—trying to get in."

"Do both happen on the same night?"

"No." She shook her head vehemently. "The person who lurks about the house is not coming from a boat. And those mornings, I don't find any signs that a boat was pulled onto the beach."

"Ever see anyone? Even a partial description is better than none?"

"A shadow, a hoodie, someone running, faceless, long legs," she recalled.

"Could it be one of the officers who's patrolling the place?"

"Absolutely not! No." She shook her head. "Most of the time, your men sit in their cars, circle around the driveway. On occasion, walk through the garden. They don't jiggle doorknobs, or sit for hours in the cold wind that comes off the ocean peering through binoculars—spying. And they are always in their police uniforms."

"They are?" he said in surprise. Then why didn't..." he stopped. No time for accusations or more questions. Not now, when she just started to open up.

"Then this morning when Barney talked about Andy's burglary, I couldn't help but wonder if that break-in had anything to do with mine and who is looking for what?" Her voice rose. "I'm the new-comer in town so every one suspects me."

He put his fingers together forming a tent under his mouth. "That's Chief Williams' reasoning, not mine. But it also raises the question what did you bring from Florida?"

"The opportunity for some people to make a lot of money. And jobs for the entire area."

He looked down at the table and smiled. "True, but no one has tried to kill Andy. And there were two attempts on your life." He looked up, caught her gaze. "We don't even know if what happened last night pertained to Megan's murder. The Zoning Commissioner is not the most popular man in town. We could be talking about two different problems. More then likely, I believe there is some sort of connection between Andy and JEC Industries. And your arrival in Whales Bay seems to have set things off."

She flashed a steely smile. "Do you really believe that? My position is such I would know if something like that existed, and I don't. Besides, isn't it strange that the town has so many attempted burglaries off season."

"Many? How many did you have, Kyra? What are you still holding back?"

She threw him a glance of sheer anger.

He leaned towards her. "You know how I work. I look at evidence—motives. I'm not rushing to blame anyone, but I need the truth."

Her skin had become moist, her hand limp. She pulled it away.

He wanted to have sex not discuss murder, his job, her job, or who said what to whom. He knew they had to stop dancing around what had happened, if anything was to come from this relationship. Tonight had been a good start, but now, all he wanted was to hold her in his arms and have sex.

He started to rise when her voice sharpened.

"Anyway, what papers were taken from McDermott's office?" His love had returned to the gathering of information.

He sat straight up in his chair, frustrated, to play her game of quid-pro-quo. "Andy said Megan brought a box of stuff with her—different types of paperwork—when she moved back into the house. Threw some in the garbage, brought the rest to his office. Neither one had a chance to look through it. She just stacked the loose papers on the end of his credenza where they stayed accumulating dust and put the box in his closet.

Recently, Andy skimmed through several manila folders that were still in the box. He said most were work related, a few property listings, and some potential clients. He decided if he couldn't get to them in a couple of days, he would bring the files into her real estate office. There was one folder though that had your name on it. He put this one on top of the papers."

Startled, she said, "What was in it?"

"Zoning ordinances pertaining to JEC Industries. However, when he looked into it this morning, the file was empty."

"I don't know what to say." She shrugged worry showed across her face.

"Andy said you stopped in yesterday. He turned his back when you requested he adjust his window blinds and that was probably when you stole the papers."

"I stole the papers! Not his so-called burglar?"

"He said the two of you were discussing Megan's file on your company's zoning ordinances. He decided to look through it after you left and saw the file was empty. Andy claims Megan's notes were taken while you were there before his office was burglarized. He also believes you could have returned after hours to grab any other data she might have left. He practically accused you of being the burglar."

"What? Now, I'm also skilled in robbing mid-rise buildings." She jumped up, started pacing back and forth. "Maybe I should go home before I'm railroaded into jail for theft and murder. Then everything in Whales Bay could go back to normal." Throwing her hands out into the air, she moved quickly around the kitchen and began clearing the table.

Tom got up, grabbed her wrist. "Kyra, stop! Talk to me. What happened in Andy's office the other day?"

"He never showed me a file," she hissed, her face flushed with fury. "Never said Megan left reports or paperwork pertaining to JEC. What he did say was that his wife mentioned discussing zoning regulations with ME, and that I should have met with him instead of her."

"And..."

"And I said there had to be a miss-understanding because I never met or saw his wife until I found her dead body. Even then, I didn't know who she was. But he reiterated Megan told him about our meeting." Kyra swallowed hard. "I didn't want to play he—said—I—said, so I made a business decision not to get into an argument at that time and dropped the entire conversation." Her eyes spilled over with tears. "Now, I feel so vulnerable. I'm a senior VP of a national corporation and not only does no one believe me, but I'm accused of all sorts of terrible things."

"I believe you, Kyra. That's what counts and why I ask." He held her upper arms sliding his fingers slowly up and down her skin. "I'll take care of every thing."

She locked eyes with his. "For me or for the VP of JEC industries?"

The nerves knotted in the back of his neck. "Kyra, keep it simple. We will get whoever is after you and who is Megan's murderer."

He reached out putting his arms around her. Felt her body taut against his, not bending. He held her tight, murmuring her name like a mantra.

She leaned into him with a soft moan.

He tilted her head kissed the tears from her face. He lingered on her lips, invaded her mouth with his tongue and she exhaled a sob.

Her breath was like an aphrodisiac. Her voice sent chills up his spine.

"Tom, I can't fight with you." She rubbed a leg against his and he lifted her up holding her hips open wide. Instantly, she wrapped her legs around him.

Moving forward, he pressed her against the Island and sat her on the top.

She felt his pants drop down. Her stomach fluttered, her breath came in shallow bursts. She reached to unzip her jeans.

He stood between her legs pulling the jeans off. She lifted herself, and her panties followed to the floor. She moaned at the touch of his bare skin.

He rubbed his hands along the inside of her thighs, moved his fingers gently into her core and climbed on top. Covering her body with his, he licked his way from her breasts down to her very being.

—⟨+ +⟩—

She rolled over to his side of the bed. Snuggled into his pillow. "Good morning."

He was standing above her buckling his belt. Leaning down he kissed her cheek. "I tried not to wake you."

"You didn't. What time is it?"

"Almost six."

"Tom, I..."

"Go back to sleep."

"There's something I have to tell you." Her voice was raspy and low.

"What?" He holstered his gun, checked his magazine, handcuffs, Taser, flashlight, and cell phone. His mind already engrossed in the coming day.

"I was very good friends with JE's girlfriend, Isabella."

He looked straight at her. A cold film was covering his eyes.

"She was murdered last October in Miami. They never found the killer."

"And?" His eyes narrowed.

"I was questioned extensively by the police."

"You never mentioned it."

"I didn't see any reason too. So many miles away, and eventually, they felt it was a burglary gone wrong. She had kept a lot of jewelry in her villa that was missing."

"What did she look like?"

"Not like me," Kyra gave a sad little laugh. She was a brunette, taller, more voluptuous. About eight years older," her voice trailed off.

"And what was your connection to each other?"

"We met once a week for lunch or dinner. We'd also take turns inviting friends over. Isabella was a great cook. She was smart, charming, and very resourceful. JE appeared quite content when he was with her."

"How long were they together?"

"About five, six years."

"Did she do any work for Mr. Cassel, or his companies?"

"No." Kyra shook her head slowly. "Some times she would throw parties or entertain business acquaintances. They would do that as a couple…" her voice trailed off.

"What?" Tom pulled the desk chair closer to the bed sat forward hands clasped between his knees.

"Chief Williams knows."

"How?"

"When I left your office, he called me in, mentioned it. Practically said I was a serial killer."

"Now you tell me?" Tom stood face flushed, the nerve beating near his jawline. His words became sharp like a razor, "Did he say how he got the information?"

"No." She burst into tears.

He leaned over cupped her face in his hand.

She turned and kissed the inside of his palm.

He swallowed a deep breath.

She felt a wave of sadness over disappointing him.

"Is there anything else, Kyra?"

"Nothing."

"Nothing for now, or nothing new until another incident comes up in the future?"

"Tom, what else could I say or do. I didn't know anyone on Cape Cod. I was on a business trip involving billions of dollars. If I would have mentioned Isabella's murder from over six months ago and sixteen hundred miles away; my entire life would have been fodder for every spin doctor, newspaper, and twitter."

He leaned over stroked a curl back from her forehead, and brushed her lips with his. "You could be right, but now we'll never know."

Walking out of the bedroom, he threw a glance at the sun rising out of the sea. Earlier, he'd awakened just before midnight. Something, a thought, a question had buzzed around his head like a bee, but wouldn't let him sleep. He heard the swell of waves pounding against the beach and got out of bed pulling the curtains open. The half moon and star-filled sky reflected on the ocean's white tipped waves. He'd picked up Kyra's binoculars lying next to his gun on the desk. It took several minutes for him to scan the horizon across the waters. He did not see a small powerboat, or someone watching the house, or watching him stand naked in Kyra's bedroom.

But it was only one night.

And now there were two murders.

CHAPTER SEVENTEEN

The day of the party the sky was blue and cloudless. The sun a golden ball high above. The balmy weather as perfect as if Kyra had placed a special order. Tom caught his breath when he entered the mansion's oversized living room.

The French doors were opened wide to the flagstone patio, sweeping beach and smooth—as—glass sea. On the horizon the sky and ocean blended in a breathtaking vista.

Kyra must be proud of a job well done, he thought. The setting worthy of the world's most prestigious beaches. She had used the view to her utmost advantage.

Most of the furniture had been removed. The well-dressed crowd divided between city cocktail and Cape Cod fashion mingled near the modern-lit bar and hot buffet stands. The party buzz ricocheted from indoor tables to those placed on the patio and under the trees. The buzz escalated each time the front doors opened and new guests arrived.

Tom glanced casually through the crowd looking for Kyra. His breath caught in his throat at the sight of her flaming red hair flowing loose and past her shoulders. She reminded him of the pictures on book jackets with far-away princesses their tresses blowing in the wind.

She wore a green silk suit, small dangling gold earrings and a jade slide that rested in the hollow of her throat. Both her plunging neckline and her hips in the pencil slim skirt captivated him. Her legs long and shapely ended in bone colored patent leather high heel pumps with platforms.

He started toward her, but in a split second she was gone. He made a slow circuit of the room. The high school principal waved and as Tom waved back, he caught a glimpse of a red head at the iced shrimp and caviar station. Moving in that direction, he saw Kyra spooning caviar on toast points while chatting with a stocky, smiling man Tom recognized from the Chamber of Commerce.

The crowd parted.

Tom pushed forward at the same time that Andy McDermott honed in on Kyra like a radar device. In a few quick steps, Rory moved past the local theatre group until she was standing face—to—face with Kyra whispering into her ear.

Kyra arched an eyebrow, started to turn when the Head Librarian brushed past, stopped in front of McDermott and handed him a Bloody Mary. She appeared to be coaxing him out to the patio. Whatever she said seemed to work for he nodded and together they moved through the opened doors sipping their drinks and laughing.

Barney muttered over Tom's shoulder, "I can't believe Kyra invited him, or that Andy actually showed up. He called her a killer and a thief at the Town Council, yet here he is drinking her liquor, eating her food...."

"Barney, the man can't be trusted," Tom interjected. "He says one thing does another and then plants innuendoes in every one's path."

"There has to be a rational reason for his behavior."

"A calculated reason that benefits him. He could be setting Kyra up for a fall."

"Tom! There's no proof."

"That doesn't seem to stop the local police."

"I have no control over that."

"You know Kyra. You've worked with her on the party. Seen her with Matt. Do you think she's capable of murdering someone?"

"No. But I don't think Andy is either. Maybe bullheaded, perhaps always looking for an angle, but a killer, no."

"Stay cool, Guys," Rory murmured taking her husband's arm. "It's party time and it won't do any good to get upset or let others see we're upset."

"She's right. Where's Kyra?"

"Someone waved and she disappeared."

"But not for long." He smelled the faint aroma of Kyra's fragrance. Felt several strands of her hair brush his cheek.

"Hi there," she said in a husky voice joining the threesome.

Tom leaned forward brushing his lips against Kyra's porcelain skin. Realizing it was the wrong thing to do, he hesitated a moment. Then followed through by kissing his sister on the cheek. "Both of you look lovely."

"The Chief doesn't approve," Rory said under her breath, smiling, while she nodded towards the bar.

"Didn't expect him either," Tom replied.

Williams seemed transfixed, his eyes riveted on them. He acknowledged Tom above the rim of his glass and turned toward a tall thin couple talking animatedly to his wife.

"Who's the couple?" Tom asked.

"Lawrence Ellridge and his secretary. Don't know if they are a couple. The invitation said with guest."

"They live on the Cape?"

"No, in Boston."

"He's a friend of yours?"

"Not really. My company uses him for legal issues from time to time that come up in Massachusetts. I was obligated."

"I wonder how he knows Williams and his wife?"

"Can't imagine." She frowned bit the corner of her lower lip. "But I should find out. It could be important. See you later."

Someone moved backwards, jarred against her. Kyra stumbled. Tom grabbed her elbow felt her body heat through his sport jacket. Felt his heart pound against his chest.

"Thanks." Clenching his arm, she settled herself, smiled, adjusted her sleeve and headed straight toward the Boston couple, the Whales Bay Chief of Police and his wife.

Tom spotted Will, over six feet tall in pressed jeans, holding his standard bottle of Samuel Adams beer and leaning against the bar surveying the room. So, despite his complaints, Will did feel he was on a job and not at a social event. Otherwise, there would have been a different drink in his hand. A Pimm's No.1 Cocktail! An old Cape Cod favorite Will still drank when he was relaxing.

The two men headed toward each other. Will's wife, Tracie met them halfway with stacked plates piled high with an assortment of party sandwiches and seafood.

"I left a drink with my jacket on a rear table. This way." She led them around the crowd, set the plates down with a handful of cocktail napkins and plastic forks.

Will had followed with an assortment of salads on a large plate that he placed in the center of the table.

"Thanks for coming, today," Tom said. "I really appreciate it. I know the two of you just finished other cases and wanted a weekend off."

Will and Tracie worked in the Boston Attorney General's office and through the years investigated several of the cases Tom had.

"I have to admit this is a great way to meet all the principals instead of working the computer or listening to co-workers. Maybe, the Governor could arrange a party like this whenever we have an unknown killer," Will joshed.

"And the food looks…tastes delicious." Tracie took a bite of a giant pawn. Her soft brown eyes opened wide in pleasure. Her auburn hair was cut in a bob and bounced each time she turned her head. Her caramel skin was already taking on a pink tinge. She wore a tailored navy pants suit and looked fit and agile. She took a sip of her diet soda, and asked, "Is Barney the caterer?"

"Yes." Tom put a forkful of lobster casserole on a plate.

"And Ms. Stevens is the red head talking to Williams?"

"Yes."

"And Andy McDermott?" Will glanced around the room.

Tom looked about. "He's outside with the Head Librarian, Charlotte Ellis. He's wearing a charcoal grey Armani suit."

"And drinks too much," Tracie added.

"You noticed?" Tom said.

"He stands out in a crowd." She paused. "Is the tall brunette in the lilac Maxi dress your sister?"

"Yes. And I'd like to know more about the couple talking to Chief Williams."

"No problem," Will said in a pensive tone. "And it also appears that Kyra does, too."

"Where's Barney?" Tom asked as he caught up to Rory about ten minutes later. "What a crowd? Someone appears and someone disappears. Almost like they're playing Hide—and—go—seek."

"A town board member hijacked Mr. Mayor. You have to move fast to keep up with him."

"I keep telling him, he has too much on his plate." Tom's eyes roamed around the room.

"Wasn't that your colleague, Will?"

"Yes, and his wife, Tracie. But I wish you wouldn't mention it for the present. I don't want to tell Kyra yet, that I brought them into the case."

"Okay. If that's the way you want to handle it. Don't you think she'll notice?"

"Maybe yes, maybe no."

Meanwhile, he didn't recognize half the guests. Several, by sight only. There was something familiar about the pretty blonde young woman who walked outside with Danny Pirro and he realized that she worked in Town Hall.

"So, that's what the Hotel Queen looks like." Hannah Rodgers said with a laugh as she slipped her arm through Tom's.

"It's good to see you, too?" Rory said looking like she was sucking on a wedge of lemon.

"If you popped up sooner, I would have introduced you." Tom glanced into the hazel eyes of the Cape's rising Assistant District Attorney.

"I'm more intrigued by Andy McDermott showing his face at the suspect's party."

Feeling the pressure of her breast against his arm, Tom side-stepped tried to act indifferent.

"When I saw him I wasn't sure you were invited." Her voice was dry and raspy.

"For a lawyer, you shouldn't pay attention to gossip," Tom said. "Only facts."

Hannah didn't flinch, gave a coy smile. "Are you making an arrest in the murder, or here to get reacquainted with all the witnesses and suspects?"

"I didn't see your name on the guest list?" Rory said pointedly.

"I came with the District Attorney and Pete. The invitation said with guest, but the D.A.'s wife couldn't make it. So, he asked Pete and me to join him. Said an extra guest wouldn't matter in such a large crowd. Anyway, the D.A. felt one of us would eventually prosecute the McDermott case and we should attend to get a glimpse of the main characters."

"How did he know how many people?" Rory asked.

"The usual way, Gossip." Hannah withdrew her arm, placed her hand on Tom's shoulder and stared into his face. "This party resembles an Agatha Christie murder mystery. Was that the effect the Hotel Queen wanted?"

Rory drew in a deep breath. "Catch up with you later," she said in an abrupt tone and disappeared into the crowd.

"Good to see you, Hannah," Tom said. "I heard you were back."

"You could have called and said hello."

He glanced at her with a skeptical expression. "I thought I was persona non gratis."

A year ago they had one drink, one dinner, one kiss and Ms. Rogers decided they were a perfect couple. When she arranged for a get—away weekend and Tom said no, she moved on to someone new. It didn't help that he had destroyed one of her cases. Proved that the defendant had an ironclad alibi.

He had heard that she was living on the mainland and there was an almost engagement. Now, she had returned—alone—renting a condo in Dennis Port.

She patted his cheek and walked off. "See you around, Tommy."

"More than likely." He ruminated over this latest development, the DA's decision of who would prosecute. He didn't believe the DA would turn such a high profile case over to an Assistant District Attorney. Taylor was definitely wetting their appetites. But as the investigation wound down he would take control.

Tom searched the crowd for Will.

People were circulating and he saw several glazed smiles. He hoped the Chief had arranged for extra patrols tonight on the narrow roads.

Before he reached the open doors, the crowd broke apart once more, and he spotted Rory chatting with Kyra who threw her head back and laughed.

"Jeez, what is Rory telling her?" Barney elbowed towards him. "Your girlfriend was standing alone greeting guests before you arrived. It would be nice if we could close the two cases before the season sets in, the sharks return from where they came from, and you stand beside Kyra at the next event."

"How do you know she's my girlfriend?" Tom asked, "And by the way, where do the sharks come from?" He nodded to a passing couple he'd noticed at Little League.

"You'd be surprised what I know. Knowledge is very important to a Mayor. Don't play it cool, Tom, don't be her good old buddy. Go for it. She's a very special lady."

"Who lives and works in Florida."

"The weather is warmer down south." Barney shook his head, scanned the happy crowd. "Has to be close to fifty people. Kyra planned on forty."

"How much food was delivered?"

"For fifty." Barney grinned. "We treated her like family."

Tom arched a brow tilted his head. "You're pushing too hard."

Kyra appeared, kissed Barney on the cheek. "Everything is delicious. Couldn't have done it without you."

"Too much kissing around here," Barney said.

They started laughing.

Kyra turned to Tom. Artic blue eyes locked with his. "Who's the girlfriend?"

Before he could say a word, Tom heard Andy McDermott's voice slurred and loud. "Do you golf, Braden?"

Tom whirled about.

The Zoning Commissioner held a fresh Bloody Mary in his hand, took two swallows, leaving the ice clicking in his glass. "We have to talk. I like to get together on the golf course out in the open. No gimmicks recording what is being said. I always considered security very important. But here I am, my wife murdered and my office burglarized. The hell with security." He raised his glass in a toast. His eyes bore into Kyra's face.

Barney grabbed him by the arm. "Let's get something to eat. Even if I have to say so myself, the food is delicious."

Tom took a sip of his Manhattan then put the half-filled glass on a strolling waiter's tray and locked eyes with Kyra. "Why did you invite McDermott?"

"When I had the meeting with him before the burglary, it seemed like a logical thing to do."

"Maybe logical, but not sensible."

Her eyebrows rose in surprise. "Sometimes you have to shake things up."

"Maybe in business, or in a TV Sitcom, but not in a murder investigation. The murder itself shook things up."

Waiters approached with finger food; giant prawns, mini pizzas and lobster quiches. Kyra took two of the little quiches, handed one to Tom, and took a bite of hers. A thoughtful expression suddenly crossed her face. "Sorry, but I just remembered I promised to chit—chat with one of my guests."

Off she went, dumping the remainder of her quiche and stopping by Bryant Cooper, the publisher of the local newspaper.

He was fussing with a slice of key lime pie moving the crust away from the filling to the amusement of a young woman in a casual jean outfit. There appeared to be an introduction. And as the women shook hands, Tom recognized Bryant's daughter, Niomi Cooper who had passed the Bar a few years ago, worked for awhile in a mid-sized Boston law firm, and had returned to Whales Bay and opened her own practice.

Tom shook his head in wonderment. It appeared that in two months, Ms. Kyra Stevens had met most of the people who ran the town.

All of a sudden, Chief Williams pushed past, spun on his heel, his eyes glued to the patio. Pent up rage creased his face. He rushed out onto the terrace and down the steps to the lawn and onto the flight of beach stairs.

Tom watched until he was out of sight.

Who the hell had Williams been talking too?

And what about?

CHAPTER EIGHTEEN

Leaning against the patio balustrade, Tom updated Will on Megan McDermott's murder and the attempts on Kyra's life.

The day had quieted down. The sun was sliding slowly toward the east leaving orange streaks in its wake. Egrets and seagulls darted in and out of the waves catching their dinners. The view was as beautiful as the earlier one and made a perfect ending for Kyra's party.

It appeared that most of the guests had left. Rory went to pick up Matt from his play date and Barney was at his restaurant preparing for the Sunday dinner crowd. Tracie had driven off to register at the Hyannis Port Motel where she and Will had reservations. The couple didn't want to stay in the middle of the Whales Bay action and preferred to be near Tom's state police office.

Mrs. Nelson supervised the catering staff that was cleaning-up the lower level of the house and grounds. Trying to stay out of their way, Tom and Will moved from room to room finally deciding to go outside for privacy.

Tom was describing the intruder's latest attempt to break into the mansion when a shrill scream cut through the balmy late afternoon.

The woman's screams rebounded up to the house from along the beach. Tom spun on his heel. He took off across the grass followed by Will. The two jumped over the gate dropping to the sand below. The squawking birds circled higher and higher in the sky.

The screaming stopped as suddenly as it started. Further along the beach, Tom could see Lily's hands covering her mouth. The breeze was lifting her skirt above the knees. He saw her footprints going backwards to where she now stood in the lacy foam at the water's edge. Shoeless, her bare feet were burrowing into the wet earth.

Danny Pirro was leaning over a body.

A man's body! A big guy!

A large knife protruded from his back. Blood spread over and around his clothes forming rivulets that ran into the sand.

Danny looked up, his face ashen as he called out, "It's the Chief."

Tom stopped dead in his tracks, thought he hadn't heard correctly. "Chief Williams?" he shouted.

Danny stood, nodded his head. "It's a bad one."

Will slowed, stopped a foot behind Tom. "Who the hell would kill him?"

Tom walked closer pulling rubber gloves out of his pockets and bent over the body. "Call it in," he hissed. "He was stabbed in the back. Did you see anyone on the beach? Old, young, male, female?"

"Earlier, when we started walking. But not on our way back."

"How long did it take you to return?"

"At least forty-five minutes."

"Make a list of who you saw. Meanwhile, we'll wait for the Medical Examiner to determine the exact time of death."

"Any wounds in his chest?" Will asked.

"Hard to tell with all the blood. I don't want to turn the body. I see at least three deep wounds. After the first one, Williams didn't have much of a chance. It probably brought him halfway down. He must have had a bad argument with someone. Angry, he turned from his assailant never expecting the knife."

"Unless there is a wound in front."

"I doubt it. Not the way the blood pooled."

"They're sending a bus and putting out a call for the Medical Examiner," Pirro interjected. "A nearby patrol car is already on its way."

Tom glanced at Lily. "Are you okay?"

"Yes. My shoes." She looked around. "I dropped them when..."

"It's okay. Ask Kyra to borrow a pair. CSI will have to go over yours anyway. We'll return them as soon as possible." Tom walked toward Pirro. "I need you to take Lily to the house and gather everyone together. Don't let anyone leave until they're questioned, even if you have to restrain them. As soon as the other men show up, I'll have them relieve you and we can go over what happened."

"Don't worry, I'll take care of everything."

Fists on hips, Tom looked from Williams' body to the white-capped waves. Shaking his head, he watched Danny murmur to Lily as they started to make their way toward the stairs.

"We better cross the Tees on this case and then some," Will said shaking his head. "A Chief of Police."

"True." Tom mumbled, moving closer to the seawall. "I'll set things in motion, make some calls."

He punched in the Governor's direct number. Told him precisely what happened then asked to arrange for several warrants.

Next, he called Whales Bay Lieutenant Pat Hendrix. Tom knew Hendrix and Williams were close. They had worked together many years. It was a difficult conversation for him to make.

Last, he phoned his office in Hyannis Port and requested the CSI team and the people he wanted to work on the case.

Hearing loud voices, Tom looked up. Danny and Lily were mid-way on the stairs. They had stopped as Kyra started down. She'd changed into jeans and a long sleeved tee shirt. From where he stood, Tom could see her say something, listen, and then grab Danny's arm.

A look of shear shock covered her face. Kyra's complexion turned as pale as the police officer's.

Mrs. Nelson, who was hurrying after Kyra, overheard and clasped a hand over her mouth. She tried pushing past Danny, but he braced himself and held his ground. Tom swore the housekeeper had tears running down her cheeks. He could hear Danny's voice rising as he held back the three women and moved them along the walkway until they disappeared from view.

The first pair of patrol officers to arrive started marking off the area with crime scene tape while a second pair went to the house to exchange places with Danny.

Tom shouting after them, "Don't let anyone, I mean anyone, leave the premises, or use the phone until I talk to them."

The CSI team who probably drove over ninety miles per hour to get there arrived on the heels of the first responding officers. Then to Tom's surprise, several patrol cars from nearby towns pulled in.

"Keep everyone back, so they don't muddy up the scene. Where's the Medical Examiner? The body has to be moved before the tide comes in."

Lieutenant Hendrix, a beefy guy with a broken nose, who had a reputation for questioning every thing, hurried over to Tom, a fire burning in his eyes. "Why are we using your CSI team and not ours? We have a good staff."

"I don't want good. They do not have enough murder experience. I want the crew licensed by the state that deals with the state's top priority cases."

"How about the Chief's wife? Is she here?"

"She left about an hour ago with another couple. Said she had a headache. Do you want to go over to their house and tell her what happened?"

"Yes and no." Pat looked Tom in the eye. "I should be the one, but I'm not leaving until the M. E. arrives."

"That's your call. He was your Chief."

"Could this murder be related to the Megan McDermott case?"

"I don't know. It doesn't appear to be. No one walks around with a Chef's knife. The murderer had to go into the kitchen, grab the knife, walk down to the beach and depending on the time, pass dozens of people."

"Is it the same knife used on Megan?" Hendrix rocked back on his heels.

"I don't think so," Tom said. "We never found the knife that killed her. Mrs. McDermott's wounds were narrower as if cut with a very sharp and smaller sized blade.

"How about the JEC Industries VP who discovered Megan. The one Williams said you were protecting? Was she here?"

"She was the hostess, it's her house up on the bluff, and I did not protect her."

Tom glared, though surprised that Hendrix didn't know about the party.

"Was Andy McDermott here?"

"Yes."

"Was he drinking?"

"As usual," Will replied.

⇌⇋

Tom sat beside Matt brushing the hair off his son's forehead. Closing the book the two had been reading, he watched Matt's face settle into a deep sleep. It had been a long day for his boy, and the buffet supper Kyra promised had to be postponed. "We will make it up. It's a deal, partner," Tom whispered walking into his own bedroom.

The flash of headlights moving up his driveway stopped him cold. Quickly, he moved to the locked drawer where he kept his gun and hurried downstairs. The car had stopped. The door opened and closed. Tom walked to the front window. It was his brother-in-law.

"Tom, it's me. Open up," Barney shouted.

"What's happening now?" Tom exclaimed.

"The town council has been bugging me for answers. They haven't stopped calling since they learned Chief Williams was killed. Could you please meet with them tomorrow?"

"No." Tom shook his head. "I'm now working on two murders and an attempted murder."

"It's April. They claim seasonal rentals are down and..."

"They never track the flow of vacationers for at least another month."

"Can't you even talk to them?"

"Another time. Not now. I don't report to the council. I report to the Governor and I can't jeopardize my cases by providing information to people who are not directly involved. They have to deal with Lieutenant Hendrix now, but if he is smart he will tell them the same thing I'm telling you. When I have something to say, it will be to you not because you are my brother-in-law, but because you are the Mayor."

"It's bad, Tom. Several of the councilmen exclaimed there is a serial killer on the loose. If the newspapers quote them..."

Tom leaned forward, hands clasped between his knees, eyes riveted on Barney's face. "It is NOT a serial killer! Perhaps, we would know more, if Williams hadn't let personal feelings get in his way, and the council itself was above board."

"What do you mean by that?"

"Secrets, real estate and money."

"What real estate? What money? No one on the council had any reason to kill Megan or the chief.

"Everyone is trying to get their hands on the old Dickerson estate."

"Aunt Vicky's property?"

"How many offers did you get during the past year?"

"At least three, but not from council members. Why?"

"Have you told Aunt Vicky?"

"No. Every few years somebody becomes interested promises great expectations and more money than we dreamed of. Phone calls, memos. Then everything falls through. Aunt Vicky is older. All these ups and downs are no good for her health. I feel it's just better to ignore the situation. At this time, none of us really need the money or the grief that accompanies acquiring it. We decided to wait it out."

"I believe the murders have something to do with the property."

"I can understand a connection with Megan. Even Andy. She was a real estate broker. He's the town's Zoning Commissioner, but how could Williams' murder be related to a deserted piece of saw—grass and sand? The beach house is unlivable. The dock needs work, lots of work. More than likely, both should be demolished."

"I'm not sure, but I don't believe in coincidences."

"That's what Kyra said."

"She spoke to you about the property?"

"At the party. Before I left. Her company is interested."

"Are you?"

"It depends on Aunt Vicky. So, now we know why Kyra is here? JEC Industries wants to buy Aunt Vicky's land for a hotel and a condo development?"

"Yes. That's true."

"Then why didn't she talk to me earlier?"

"Until recently, I don't believe she knew you were related to the Dickerson's. You were just Barney." Tom shook his head. Plastered a smile on his face.

⌐+⌐

Kyra prowled the house checking the doors, windows, and alarm before returning to her room and scanning the beach. She stood behind her bedroom's half drawn drapes watching the scene unfolding down below.

At dusk, the police had installed lights that lit up the murder scene like it was a sunny day at noon. Then Kyra turned on her outside lights as much for her own peace of mind as to help the police.

She had watched as a truck left tracks on JE's white sandy beach delivering sacks of dirt. The police used them to build a temporary seawall that would hold back the tide.

Kyra started shaking as Williams' body was taken away.

A couple of officers started patrolling the area from the bend, past the back of the house and the Sullivan Compound, and then returning to the crime scene.

The CSI men used mag lights to canvas the ground inch by inch and had already left. Against the walls of a huge tent, Kyra could make out flickering shadows that bounced across the water.

Tom had disappeared. He had phoned from his car telling her not to worry. He would see her tomorrow morning.

Not worry! She felt as if she was caught and thrown about in a whirlpool not of her choosing.

She squeezed her JE phone hoping it would ring. She had phoned James Enrico earlier, but he hadn't returned her call. And as the clock ticked away, her nerves were spinning out of control.

He wasn't carrying their lifeline, as he used to put it. Up to a month or so ago, he never went anywhere without his phone that he used strictly for Kyra's number.

Taking in a deep breath, she pressed redial again.

In an instant, JE picked up immediately. "What's happening?"

"There's been another murder."

"Who?" His voice, angry and cold, touched every nerve in her body.

"The town's Chief of Police."

"Williams?"

"Yes?"

"Where?"

"On the beach. Close to the bend, near the big rock where the land turns."

"At the end of my property line, or on the other side."

"On your land."

"Jeez! My God! Disastrous. Soon they'll be calling my place the Murder House. They're not holding you responsible? Are they?"

"No." She held her breath not really knowing.

"Perhaps this time you have a good alibi?"

"Yes. I was playing hostess with the movers and shakers of Whales Bay."

"Thank God. My name and the company's name must be kept out of this one."

She couldn't answer. Didn't respond. She was positive half of the town held her and JEC Industries responsible for everything that went wrong with their lives.

"Should I send Alessandro up there?"

"No. It would send the wrong signal." She couldn't breathe till he answered. A cramp sliced across her stomach.

"True." He paused. "What does your Lieutenant have to say about his rogue killer?"

"He's not my Lieutenant!" She heard his dry chuckle.

His voice took on a sarcastic tone. "Are we any closer to getting bids on the heart of the Whales Bay land?"

"Yes. I'm in contact with the people from the Dickerson Trust."

"What?" His voice roared bounced against her eardrum.

"Yes," she repeated solemnly.

"How did this happen? I thought the Dickerson owners couldn't be found and I was never told about a TRUST." A perplexed tinge of disbelief shaded his words.

"It's what I've been working on. Good research and contacts," she said. "You know, once I get started, I always deliver for you, JE." Kyra couldn't help giving herself a little pat on the shoulder. So, Mr. Ellridge was going behind her back to James Enrico and telling him the same lies he had told her. "Oh and by the way, the party was a great success. You would have enjoyed it. I'll forward some pictures for your perusal."

JE hadn't called. Didn't ask. Why? He usually liked all sorts of tidbits. Who drank what? Who wasn't dressed appropriately? And who made a faux pas?

"There was just one strange thing," she said, trying to contain her nerves.

"And what was that?" He sounded put off, his mind already concentrating on another tangent. Perhaps questioning other stories repeated to him by the real estate lawyer. Wondering which ones were true?

"Ellridge and his colleague seemed very friendly with Chief Williams and his wife. They spent the entire afternoon drinking together. I hope this murder doesn't raise questions and delay things just when they are starting to take off."

CHAPTER NINETEEN

*H*e stared unseeing across the parking lot toward his pick-up truck, the lone vehicle at the motel.

He needed to call his boss, knew he had to convince the man he had nothing to do with stabbing the Chief of Police and had no idea who did. He felt it was imperative that he ignored the newspapers and spin doctors who were trying to connect the two murders.

Did the boss hire another hit man to kill the Chief because he had killed the wrong woman? If so, then there would be no money, all his plans destroyed, and he would have to get out of town.

Could he blame it on a copycat? Someone, who had a motive other than money?

Simple enough, he could say. He crashed the party. Had a couple of drinks, a sandwich (pretty damn good) and no one the wiser. He acted like he belonged and it worked. There must be someone angry enough with a Chief of Police who could wield a blade and imitate the decade's Cape Cod murderer.

Maybe his boss already knew who the killer was?

He would tell the truth. That he planned on returning later that night after the party. Felt the lady would be exhausted; turn in early with no guests. Then he would finish the job started in March and GET HIS MONEY! Damn!

Every thing had worked against him. Now, he had to stay away from the shoreline, couldn't be spotted spying on the mansion high on the bluff. No way could he break in while the Police were patrolling front and back.

God—didn't Ms. Kyra Stevens look great in green?

CHAPTER TWENTY

B y Tuesday morning, Hendrix had the Whales Bay police check all the motels on the Cape. There was one located off Route Six in Sandwich where a male guest had stayed for the past month.

But the man had left The Bed & Coffee on Saturday, the day before the party. Said he was disappointed with the fishing and now the shark sightings and decided to go home.

The manager told the officer that the man, Al Morgan, had slept in most mornings and stayed out most nights except for a week or so when he was sick.

Will was surprised that if it was Kyra's assailant, or Williams' murderer why didn't the stranger switch motels more often.

Tom thought Morgan—if that was his name—might have been afraid that if he constantly moved around during off-season, he would leave a trail crisscrossing the Cape. He probably figured it would be safer staying put than moving about.

Thinking the man might not have bothered with a disguise when he was ill, or had altered his appearance upon leaving, Tom asked the police artist to see the Bed & Coffee Manager.

He hoped the Manager remembered something that added to the artist's original sketch drawn from Kyra's description. That first sketch was based on her memory of the assailant's eyes and tip of his nose.

The motel manager mentioned that Morgan kept to himself and he rarely saw him except when he paid cash for his weekly bill. But Tom knew, any clue, no matter how insignificant could affect the entire case.

The physical description fit almost anyone, five foot seven—to—nine, on the slim side, brown hair covered by a baseball cap and sunglasses. He spoke low in short sentences, and the manager was positive he detected a slight Texan drawl. He said the man drove a dirty red pick-up truck with mud-splattered license plates, impossible to see the state. Nor did he show a license when he registered, not that the manager cared.

But the height and weight matched the description Kyra gave of the assailant who broke into her bedroom. And Tom didn't believe he had left the Cape. It was easy to rent a room this time of the year, and more important, Tom felt the suspect was a contract hit man who didn't finish what he was hired to do. He would want his money, and Tom knew he wouldn't get it while Kyra was alive.

That could account for the bungled attempts on her life and why he hung around.

Tom's determination to keep Kyra out of harm's way became his mantra, enveloping his thoughts and his very being.

He sent his CSI team over to the motel to re-process the room, assigned two of his people Clare and Ryan to find Al Morgan, no matter what it took. He didn't know if this would help find the Chief's murderer, but it could lead to Megan's killer and Kyra's assailant.

Then Will learned Williams had his men check only the hospitals on the Cape for the wounded shooter. Will took it upon himself to drive to each hospital on the mainland within a fifty-mile radius.

Midway between the Cape and Plymouth, in a small regional hospital, Will found a man with a bullet wound who checked into

Emergency the same day of the boat shooting and left after being treated.

"Fits the description, you gave," Will said to Tom over the phone. "And he listed a Boston address that the hospital has since discovered doesn't exist."

"Did he pay with a credit card?"

"No. Sorry, it was cash."

"Where was the wound?"

"In the left shoulder. And the caliber was the same as your gun."

After a moment, Tom said, "We can't seem to get a break. Did he say how it happened?"

"According to the Doctor, the patient had absolutely no idea where the shot came from."

"Bullshit! Did the hospital report the incident to the local police?"

"Of course, but by the time the police arrived the patient had checked out."

"How about paperwork?"

"He ignored some of the questions, scribbled answers to others and left an eligible signature. The best I could make out for a name was Pete Smith. Probably, another misnomer."

"If Williams had followed through when he was supposed to, we would have found this guy, and its even possible Williams might still be alive." Tom paused, his mind wandering. "Did Hendrix let you go through the McDermott murder book and computer?"

"Surprisingly, yes. But he won't hear any badmouthing about the Chief."

"That's understandable. Was there any talk at the station that the murder could be personal? Any gossip about Williams and his personal life?"

"The usual. Someone he sent to prison whose family swore was innocent and just got released. But even that was vague."

"I can't figure out why he honed in on Kyra as the killer. It never made sense. At the time of Megan's murder, Kyra wasn't on the Cape.

She has a good job. Was never in New England prior to this trip. Plus, she was here on business that would benefit the town financially.

I thought Williams was blaming her in an attempt to protect the guilty party. But the only suspect I could come up with was Andy. And he checked out. Spent the day with his girlfriend, a perfect alibi."

"Also, an excellent motive. Especially, since Megan knew about the affair and had told her parents."

"At first I believed that, but the further we investigated, the cleaner Andy got. Actually, he convinced the town council that he was unhappy at home and found a woman who truly understood him. Andy even had my brother-in-law believing him. So, if not McDermott, then who?"

"A hit man hired by him," Will said in a satisfied tone. "Or the Zoning Commissioner's girl friend, Charlotte Ellis, the Library Director."

"Great. If we can prove it." Tom was silent for a moment. "We need a lead and we need to get the bullet. CSI can identify if the bullet came from my gun. In case you need a warrant, I'll have one faxed."

"Are you thinking about two different murderers?"

"It might sound ridiculous, but maybe three."

"Three hit men?"

"Megan, Williams and two attempts on Kyra's life. That's an awful lot of killing. And someone is getting desperate and we really don't know why."

"It sounds like a television detective series."

"But who is footing the bill?"

⚑ ⚐

"I'm sorry, Mrs. Williams, but I don't have any new information." Tom leaned forward hands clasped between his knees eyes focused on the Chief's wife.

He was startled when she opened the door to the rambling grey ranch house a few minutes earlier and he saw Hendrix across the living room seated in an oversized EZ chair facing the TV. A drink was at his fingertips on a side table, his jaw set, and his expression unyielding.

Recalling prior conversations with the Chief, Tom was positive the chair was Williams' favorite. A dozen new questions conjured up to the front of Tom's mind. A widow should be annoyed that a co-worker sat in her dead husband's chair before the wake was planned and the body not released.

After introducing Tracie, Tom moved a barrel chair closer to where Mrs. Williams sat on the sofa.

She was a tall attractive woman with black hair twisted into a French knot. Her manicured nails toyed with her wedding ring, turning it around and around her finger; dark circles underlined bloodshot hazel eyes.

Tracie was sitting in the sofa's matching chair. Tom heard her bracelets jingle as she took out a pen and small notebook and started jotting down notes.

Without turning her head, Mrs. Williams shifted her glance in Tracie's direction and pursed her mouth.

As if on cue, Pat Hendrix said, "Janine called said you were coming over and asked me to be here. I didn't think you would mind. She felt uncomfortable when you said you were bringing an investigator. Especially, when the two of us had already discussed Sunday's events."

"But not with me," Tom said matter of factly ignoring Hendrix. "Mrs. Williams, I need to go over several details about Sunday. We need a timeline."

"I'll do whatever I can to help."

"I noticed the Chief was very angry when he rushed out of the party about four o'clock. Do you know why?"

Janine shook her head no.

"Mam," Tracie said in a determined tone. "Would you please respond verbally?"

Throwing a quick glance at Hendrix, Janine Williams snapped, "I have no idea why he was so angry."

"Who was your husband talking too?" Tom continued.

"Just… the three of us," Jeanne said modulating her voice.

"Who were the three?" Tom asked, knowing full well, but wanting to get their names into the notes, so he would have cause to question Ellridge at a later time.

"Friends of Reed; Larry Ellridge and his colleague, Marion Clark and myself. They went to college with Reed at Northeastern University."

"Always stayed in touch?"

"Yes."

"Did the four of you arrive at the party together?"

"Tom, is all this necessary?" Hendrix interjected. "The Doctor put Janine on medication and I can answer all of your questions. She should be resting." Flexing his hands, the Lieutenant started to rise.

"You know better, Pat. If you have to be someplace, and running late, please go. But Mrs. Williams has a lot of answers I need to continue my investigation."

Tom turned in her direction. "I don't know what the problem is, but if you are not comfortable here in your home going over the details leading to your husband's murder, we can do this at my office in Hyannis Port. Reed was viciously murdered. And I intend to find out who and why?"

"I'm as good as I can be any where," she said in a hushed tone, her shoulders sloping. "Larry and Marion picked me up about two. Reed had to stop at the station and drove himself. He arrived at the party about a half hour after us."

"Where do Ellridge and Clark live?"

"In Boston. Reed has been so busy it was difficult for us to get away. He was happy that Larry and Marion were also invited, so we could see each other."

"Reed was furious when he left," Tom said. "He rushed out, complexion flushed—almost purple. What happened?"

"I don't know. We were discussing renting a boat, the four of us, and sailing down to Florida on the Inter Coastal, late Spring, when…"

"Have you been in Florida before?"

"Of course."

"Where?"

"Miami. That's where I grew up."

"Family and friends still there?"

"My sister and…what does this have to do with Reed's murder?"

"I'm not sure, but we have to know why he was so furious when he left the party. He was killed soon after."

"He got a call on his cell phone," she said in an abrupt high-pitched tone.

"You didn't tell me," Pat Hendrix interjected his anger flashing again.

Tom glared at the officer then swiveled about. "Did your husband say who phoned?"

"No. But now that you mentioned it, I remember he did look annoyed. Said it was an emergency and he had to respond."

"Where is his phone?" Tom asked positive CSI had taken it off the Chief's belt and kept it as evidence.

"Reed was talking on it as he walked away. It was the last time I saw him," her voice cracked, eyes welled with tears. "It's already been a couple of days. Does any one outside of Pat have any idea who the killer is?"

"Lieutenant, who do you feel stabbed the Chief?" Tom asked standing with fists on his hips, anger coloring his face red.

"I feel it's connected to Megan McDermott's murder. Find her killer and you have the Chief's."

"I don't believe that," Janine blurted out.

"A possibility there's a connection, but I don't believe it either," Tom said, but he wondered.

It was a question he'd been thinking about and mentally answering for two days, a dead woman and a dead man.

There was no evidence, just a detective's instinct, each scenario vying with the other.

⚔️

Kyra got home about six tired and hungry. She was thinking about how much she accomplished while at the same time deciding on what she should tell JE and Tom.

Tom who never leaves her thoughts from one day to the next.

He had said he would see her in the morning, but didn't show up, didn't phone. And she missed him. Wanted to be held. Worried about what was happening. Anxiety flooded her insides. Would she stay awake another night counting the hours?

What would it be like when she returned to Florida? Weeks or months could go by with only telephone calls, e-mails, perhaps Skype.

Get a grip on yourself, woman.

She put her tote and groceries on the kitchen table, took off her jacket and hung it on a coat hook in the mudroom. Noticing an envelope on the floor, she picked it up flicking the corner as she returned to the kitchen.

Opening the refrigerator door to start putting the dairy products away, she heard a movement on the floor above. She stopped short. Her muscles tightened, her breath came in short puffs while her eyes followed the creaking footsteps moving about upstairs.

Kyra jumped forward picked up a large frying pan dangling from the rack above the sink. Slowly, she moved to the foot of the stairs. Someone was now in her bedroom.

Should she run for it?

Were the cops still circling the house?

Her heart pounded against her chest.

The bedroom shower started.

A murderer wouldn't stop and take a shower before attacking unless he didn't want to leave his DNA.

Was it Tom?

Did JE send Alesandro, after all?

Would she have to share the house with him? His cigars? His wine?

She started up the stairs.

That's it, one step at a time. She swung the frying pan in rhythm to her steps and moved into the bathroom. She dropped the pan on the floor.

Through the frosted glass she could see the width of the broad shoulders, the long legs, the flat buns and she pulled her tee over her head, pushed out of her sneakers, slipped off her jeans and panties, dropped her bra on the tiles as she stepped into the shower.

And Tom turned, taking her into his arms.

CHAPTER TWENTY-ONE

Afterwards, they lay entangled in the huge bath sheets Tom had wrapped around them when he carried her to bed.

"What are you thinking?" he murmured into her ear as he lazily played with the curl that dangled across her cheek.

"If I should shower now or after I take out the party leftovers and we eat."

His laughter made her laugh, too. She stretched languidly thinking of how he soaped her under the flowing water, and then sucked on her breasts. He was so tender and gentle, his fingers sliding tantalizingly into her stroking the spot that drove her crazy.

When he lifted her, spreading her thighs around his body, she clung, pressed, and grabbed hold of him not wanting to let go as he entered her. JE, Alessandro, and Williams were forgotten. She was alone with Tom under the spraying water, the rest of the world gone.

Now, she cuddled into him not wanting anyone or anything to end their precious time together.

"I didn't want to wait another day. I thought I would go crazy if I didn't see you tonight." He gave a shy smile. "I haven't felt like this in years, since I was a teen—ager." He cradled her body with one hand and with the other fondled a breast. "You are so beautiful," he murmured. "Smooth and soft, so smart, I can't believe I'm the one that's lucky enough to hold you."

She lifted her head and gently kissed him on his cheek. "Everything feels so good when I'm with you. It makes me think I'm young and falling in love." She kissed him closed her eyes, couldn't believe what she had just said. Couldn't remember saying it to another man. Unconsciously, she drew away, emitted a long sigh.

"Don't be sorry you said it," he murmured as if reading her mind. He gripped her arms, and then wrapped her in his. His voice husky with emotion, "I don't have to think about it. I know I love you. This will work, Kyra. I've waited a long time and I don't want to lose you. When we're apart I worry about what's happening, if you are okay."

"Don't. I can take care of myself." She wanted to kick herself, bit down on her tongue in frustration.

"I didn't mean…you have to understand."

"I know. It's nerves. Please, don't push me."

"I didn't intend too." He cupped her cheek with his hand, ran his thumb across her lips. His hard solid body pressed into hers. The stubble of his beard as he nibbled his way down her belly, sent tingles up and down her spine.

She heard herself moan.

And he was inside, moving ever so slow and gentle, then faster and faster.

Her body matched its rhythm to his.

She arched her back and screamed.

Tom walked out of the bathroom, a towel wrapped around his middle, and picked up the frying pan brandishing it like a trophy. "Is this taking the place of the welcoming cocktail?"

"Just about. When I heard footsteps upstairs and…"

"All you could think about were two murders in the house where you live. Would it help, if you moved in with me? You know how I feel that you're alone way out here on the shore."

"I don't need a baby sitter, Tom. I'm just not used to coming home from work and finding a man in my shower. Anyone would be frightened."

"Of course. Next time, I'll call. After all, you could have had other plans." He stared at her telegraphing a silent message. Please don't do this. "Are we going back to the beginning? Feeling each other out and starting anew?"

"I don't have too." An ache pressed against her midriff. Whatever caused it rolled up into her chest? Why had she spoiled the evening that began so great? She had to fix it, before their words took off and formed their own scenario. "Anyway," she continued softly. "Outside of business, I don't make plans with other people." She forced herself not to sound sulky. She tried making a joke. "Besides which, how's your business going? Any new info?"

His distress showed he didn't get it, or wanted too.

Then in an instant, they both smiled. She got off the bed and slipped into her robe.

He pulled on his briefs and pants. "We'll get better at this," he said.

"I thought we were pretty good."

He chuckled. Tousled her hair. "See what I mean."

He took her hand walking downstairs. "I found out how Chief Williams knew Ellridge. They went to college together along with Marion Clark. They've been friends ever since."

"Who would have known? Thank you for telling me. I went to chat with them because I was curious if their relationship had anything to do with my job. They seemed so comfortable with each other that I was suspicious. But by the time I circled the room, Williams was gone and so was Ellridge."

"Ellridge, too?" Tom halted mid-step.

"Yes." She looked up at him surprised at his reaction.

"That's not what Mrs. Williams said."

Kyra shot him a glance. "Well that's what happened. She introduced me to Marian Clark, whom I already met. So, it was just we three girls."

Tom curled his lips together in a nasty grimace. She saw the nerve beating along his jawline.

"You're saying she lied?" he asked matter of factly.

"I'm saying that when I chatted with Janine and Marion at the party, Lawrence Ellridge was not there and the conversation centered on spring clothes. No matter how I tried to change the topic. And believe me, I tried."

"And Chief Williams?"

"Janine said I just missed him. He went out for a smoke and would be back shortly. I don't remember seeing him return, nor do I remember seeing him leave the party with other guests that most smokers like to do. Is that important?"

"Absolutely. He was killed about thirty—to—sixty minutes later. We need to know where everyone was, so we can start eliminating people. If Mrs. Williams lied once, what else is she lying about?"

"Do you think Ellridge is the murderer?" She stared at him open mouthed. Not in her wildest imagination had she supposed that? She pictured JE's reaction and swallowed hard.

"A possibility, or he saw the murderer and didn't realize it, or knew who Williams was meeting and didn't tell us."

"But why wouldn't he say something to the police? The way you put it the two men were friends for years?"

"I don't know. Everyone has ulterior motives."

"But we will find out? Won't we?" She tilted her head, eyes riveted to his.

Tom leaned over kissed her forehead, handed her the frying pan, and pulled his phone from his belt. Pressing a button, he spoke fast and quickly, "Will, please call Janine Williams ask her to be at the Hyannis Port office tomorrow morning at nine."

He listened for a moment. "I want to know why she lied about Ellridge's comings and goings? And if she threatens that she's bringing a lawyer, or her friend Hendrix, tell her only the lawyer will be allowed to sit in. I want her there, no matter what. If you have too, threaten with a warrant, or tell her you'll pick her up in a police car. The head of the police department was killed. His death is not going away. She has to realize we're State, work for the Governor and not local politicians."

Tom raised an eyebrow. "Doesn't matter. We'll discuss it in the morning. And I need Tracie and her notes. Let's meet at eight. I'll bring the coffee and donuts." He gave a wide grin. "Okay. Okay. I've heard it before."

He looked past Kyra's shoulder. Chewed on his lower lip. Seemed to reach a decision. "Then call Ellridge's office," he said. "Set up appointments with him and his assistant, Marion Clark for one thirty."

He listened a moment before answering. "I don't care if he is an attorney. Remind him this is a State Case. If he has to cancel a previous appointment, or a court date, tell Ellridge he has about eighteen hours to do so. We'll drive to Boston together, but we talk to them separately. And bring Tracie. I need notes taken, written or taped, but she should be prepared for either. We'll play it by ear."

He put his phone back on his belt. Walking into the kitchen he put his arm around Kyra's shoulder and helped to set out some containers and plates.

"You sounded very official," she said.

"I am. It's part of my job."

She gave a half smile, took out a couple of forks and knives from the flatware drawer, and forced the words out of her mouth, "The police took my knife rack as evidence."

"Two large wood handled knives were missing from the slots. We were hoping for fingerprints."

"Did you find any?" Her cheeks flushed bright pink.

"No. It was wiped clean. It shouldn't have been."

"I noticed two empty slots Sunday evening."

"The knives were there after Megan's murder. I checked. My CSI team checked. But now, a second stabbing and two slots are empty."

"Were my kitchen knives used to stab either one?" she whispered.

"Not Megan. We still don't have the weapon that was used to cut her throat."

"And Williams?"

"The M.E. said he was killed with the Chef's knife from the set. It was still in his back and matched the set in the kitchen."

"And the second knife that's missing?"

"Don't know."

"I want to be sure I understand this. You're saying the killer was at my party where he stole at least one knife."

"Yes."

"But how could he steal the largest knife, walk out of the kitchen and kill the Chief of Police on the beach? There were people milling about. In the kitchen, the living room, the terrace," her voice rose.

Tom stood behind her gently massaged her shoulders. "Right now, it looks that way."

"But how? He had to hide them. The blades were sharp and huge. He had to walk out of the house, across the patio and garden and down to the beach. Someone must have seen him."

"Or he could have had help." Tom turned her around lifted her on to the counter placing a hand on each side of her hips. Controlling himself not to open her robe, her thighs. Trying to have a conversation explaining his job and his ideas, trying to establish a repour with this woman who meant so much to him.

"An accomplice?" Her eyes roamed across his face, searching, studying for answers.

"It's all part of an investigation."

He kissed the tip of her nose. "Let's eat. Please. All I had since breakfast was coffee." He lifted her down moved toward the table. "By the way, Will asked why Mrs. Nelson was so upset when she heard about Chief Williams? Were they friends?"

"She was crying. Said their families knew each other for years. She liked him. Thought he ran a great police department. Definitely resented you and your team. One afternoon though, she had mentioned how he was different years ago before the Cape was built up and so many seasonal people bought property to build condos."

"Like JE wants too?"

"Yes." Kyra shrugged, threw him a glance.

"And what did she say about Ellridge?"

"Ellridge? She never mentioned him. But she did complain about the mess your men left Sunday after searching downstairs; the kitchen, dining room and the grounds. Between that and William's murder, she says she doesn't want to return. No matter how much JE pays."

"Tell her it won't look good for her not to."

Kyra gasped, sank into her chair. "You can't think…"

"Do you have a resume or paperwork on Mrs. Nelson?"

"No." Surprised, she shook her head in bewilderment. "She personally works for JE. Maybe my company has records. They usually keep them. Do you want me to call the Human Resource Department in Florida and see what they have?" She held her hands out wide.

"Tracie is taking care of that. But I thought that if…"

"I had no idea you would call…" She swallowed her words a shiver touched every nerve in her body. "Who have you or Tracie spoken too at Corporate?"

Please say no one, her heart screamed.

"I haven't. My staff has."

"I wish you would have told me."

"Why? It's protocol. We gather as much information as we can to check out alibis and motives."

"On me. You checked my alibi and motive. Called the company I work for asking questions."

"In March, I had to find out who you were. Who I was talking too? Verifying what you told me. We were strangers and a dead woman was lying on your dining room floor."

"Point well taken. At the time, you did say I was a suspect? Is that what you said to my company?" Things started to make sense, to fall into place. JE's attitude and what he said since she flew up from Florida.

"Absolutely not! We just verify people's positions, travel destinations, etc. We know what to say when we do this, Kyra. It's not a calamity..."

"Almost like checking a resume, as if I applied for a position with another company? It was my job you interfered with. And I didn't know Megan. We weren't even on the Cape together." She swallowed her words. "Maybe we moved too fast." Her nails keeping time with a staccato beat as she tapped the rim of her plate.

He swore under his breath. In two steps he was at her side. "What did you expect me to do, Kyra? I'm a cop."

"And a very good one." She stared into his face. "Maybe I was na-ive, but I never thought.... I was completely unaware." She envisioned the hornet's nest. The buzz his questions must have evoked. Did he reach JE? Did the Chairman inform the Board of Directors? Or did everything stay within Human Resources? Somehow she doubted it especially if Alessandro was involved.

Tom leaned over traced the shape of her face with his thumb. Ran his hand through her mass of curls, still moist with perspiration from their lovemaking, smoothed the hair off her forehead. "Don't be angry with me." He knew if he pressed any harder, she would press back. He didn't want an argument to end their night.

"Let's eat." She repeated his earlier words, adding, "Would you like some wine? Several opened bottles are in the refrigerator door." She rubbed the side of her neck. The next time, she had to pay more attention to what she said to JE.

And her cop lover!

CHAPTER TWENTY-TWO

By seven o'clock the next morning, Tom pulled into Rory's driveway to spend some time with Matt before the school bus arrived.

"Hungry?" Rory said as Tom kissed her cheek.

"Nah. I have a meeting with Will and Tracie and promised to bring breakfast."

"You promised to bring coffee and donuts."

"You've been talking to Tracie?"

"No. I just know you and my husband."

"Where is he?"

"He got in late last night. The Town Council is really giving him a hard time. So, Matt and I decided to let him sleep in this morning. We are being extra quiet."

"Then I'll grab Matt before he bounces down the stairs."

"How's Kyra?"

"Shaken up."

"Can you get her to move into your house?"

"She says she doesn't need a baby sitter."

"I don't think you had that in mind."

"True, but she's so upset I don't want to argue."

"Will she stay with me?"

"You can try and ask. I'd appreciate it."

Tom took the stairs two at a time stopping at his son's closed door. Knocking softly, he walked in.

Matt was swinging a new baseball bat.

"Hi Dad, isn't it cool? And my initials are engraved around the rim."

"Uncle Barney bought it?"

"Nah, Kyra did. Said it was a reward for doing so great at practice."

"She's been coming over?"

"Yeah, but she said it was a secret. So, I couldn't tell you."

"Really?" Tom wasn't sure if he liked the idea of his son having secrets behind his back. He had to think about this.

He was so caught up in his job and with Kyra, he forgot about the consequences. His son had become friends with a murder suspect who had turned into a victim, a victim who was randomly threatened.

Was he crazy to have pulled her into his personal life?

And then, involve her in Rory and Matt's lives, too? Yet, even he had just agreed that he would be pleased, if Rory would ask Kyra to stay with her and Barney. Most people in town knew their house was a second home to Matt.

And what did the killer know?

But he knew better, had ignored the consequences.

His son and sister might be caught in the line of fire? Innocent targets.

His thoughts spun like a kaleidoscope in his head.

Yet, deep down he was glad Kyra was keeping her promise. He was happy she wanted to be with his family—BUT!

These murders had to be solved. The criminals caught. He had to end it-soon. Kyra had to understand. Not just her job was on the line. So were his family's lives.

"Let's see how quietly we can go downstairs. Uncle Barney is still sleeping."

"Aunt Rory said she's making pancakes."

"And I saw the batter."

He lifted Matt to his shoulders and carried him down the steps.

Striding into the kitchen, Tom crouched near the table, so Matt could slide down, as he asked his sister, "Did you know about the secret?"

"Of course."

"How many times has Kyra come over and practiced with him?"

"Not many. About every ten days or so. You're not angry? Are you?" She glanced over her shoulder arching her brows toward Matt. "It was a surprise for you, so we couldn't say anything."

"Then I won't mention it to Kyra."

"Great idea."

"Yeah Dad. Anyway she's your friend."

"So, she is Son. So she is, though I do think she wants to be yours, too."

"Yeah, she does, and she plays great baseball for a lady."

Rory laughed. "Matt, why don't you get your history report out of the backpack to show to Dad?"

She placed a stack of pancakes on the table. Took several with funny faces made with chocolate chips and arranged them on Matt's plate.

She sank slowly into a chair. Her eyes caught Tom's.

Something was in her craw and he didn't think it had anything to do with baseball, or his love life. "Go ahead, Matt. I'd like to see it," he said. "Just be as quiet as possible." He watched his son hurry out of the room. "He never kept a secret from me before."

"It's just the first of many."

"That's why I..."

"Tom, forget it. Everyone meant well. And Matt wanted to surprise you." She hesitated a moment. "There's something else, isn't there? You once told me, cops don't give out phone numbers and addresses. I got too friendly, went to far. Now, there's a second murder."

"I started the relationship, Rory, not you. I'm the one who has to fix it."

"The two of you got along so well. Not since Ivy...I."

"And the two of us will take care of it. What else are you so worried about?"

"Williams murder and Hendrix riling up the Town Council."

"He's still at it?"

"Yes. Every day, he causes another situation. Barney believes he wants Williams' job."

"Of course he does! As Barney says, Hendrix wants to be Chief of Police so bad he can taste it. He wants to influence the Council before they interview for an out-of-town replacement."

He glanced over at his sister. "But, why does this worry you so? Did Barney and Hendricks get into a bad argument?"

"No. Nothing like that."

"Then what?"

"Something happened a couple of weeks ago that I figured was none of our business, so I didn't mention it, but I did mention it to Barney. He laughed it off. Said there could be various reasons, for what I saw. However, now that Chief Williams was murdered, I think it is very important for you to know. It might have had something to do with his death."

"What?" Tom sat down.

His sister's eyes locked with his. Her expression was too serious for idle gossip.

Worried, he grabbed her hand. "Rory, what did you see?"

"Last month, after our Festivity meeting broke up, I left with Janine Williams. Niomi Cooper stopped us—she's a newcomer on the committee—to ask some questions. Janine said she had an appointment and had to leave. So, I stayed a few minutes and filled in Niomi.

Afterwards, I went to pick up something for Barney. I stopped at the small strip mall at the edge of town. Janine's car was parked in a nearby spot and she was sitting there when I arrived. I was just about to beep my horn, when a SUV pulled in. I saw Janine get out of her car and hurry to the SUV instead of going into a store."

"And?"

"She got into the SUV and the driver pulled out."

"Who was he?"

"Pat Hendrix."

CHAPTER TWENTY-THREE

An hour later, Tom paced his office as he related Rory's story about Janine Williams to his two investigators.

"Could the Chief have been so blind?" Tracie asked taking a second donut.

"My thoughts exactly."

"Are we going to discuss this with the widow?" Will asked.

"What do you think? That is, if she shows up."

"Have some patience," Will said. "She's probably memorizing Hendrix's instructions on what to say and what not to say." His head snapped sideways at the phone's sudden ring.

Tom reached over to grab the receiver, listened for a second and smiled, "Send—HER—in," he said hanging up. "Strong woman. Ready to take on the police and investigators without a lawyer or lover at her side."

Attitude was written across Janine Williams' face and in her stance when she entered Tom's office.

Vicky, Tom's secretary, stood behind Janine and gave him a high five. Grabbing the door, she closed it as her lips mouthed, "Good Luck."

Mrs. Williams wore a black suit and high heel pumps. Her hair was twisted into the obligatory French knot. Her makeup looked perfect, though her eyes were still bloodshot and wary as she glanced around the room.

Without an invitation, she sat down in the closest chair to the door and crossed her legs refusing Tracie's offer of coffee or a donut.

"I didn't come for breakfast or chit chat. I'm here because of your official demand. The next time my lawyer will accompany me."

"I hope there won't have to be a next time. I'm investigating your husband's murder and need to know why you lied to me."

"About what?" Her eyes flashed.

Tom nodded at Tracie, who flipped her small pad open and proceeded to read several questions and answers from their first interview in the William's home.

"Your words," Tracie quoted. "Drew received a phone call, leaving Ms. Clark, Mr. Ellridge, and myself talking. He then rushed out of the party disappearing from view."

"So?"

"Mr. Ellridge was already gone when your husband got the phone call and had left your little group."

"I...I. Are you implying Lawrence disappeared outside of the house and murdered his best friend?"

"No. I'm insinuating you lied about Drew's best friend's whereabouts at the time of his murder."

"Is that what this meeting is all about? A slip of the tongue! It was the day after Drew was killed. I was upset and nervous. Simply forgot. For all I know, Lawrence had to run to the bathroom."

"I explained the importance of the timeline and had to know where everyone was so I could pinpoint the guilty party."

"Mrs. Williams, what did you think this morning's meeting was about?" Will's question hung in the air.

Janine's hand twisted the straps on her purse.

"How long have you and Pat Hendrix been involved?" Tom interjected realizing why she came alone and knowing he was throwing her off balance. "You are worried, aren't you, about your lover's alibi?"

Her eyes riveted to his. Her voice became deep and throaty. The words coated in venom. "Pat didn't kill Drew. Neither did Lawrence. More than likely, someone arrested and sentenced for a previous crime was vindictive enough to get even and kill the Chief of Police."

"We have taken that under consideration among other things. If something like that did happen, we will know very soon."

"People seem to think there is a serial killer in Whales Bay," Janine blurted out. "They want to know who could be next on the murderer's list? Who is going to be number three? Drew's men are taking turns watching my house. I wouldn't be surprised if one of them followed me here. They are worried. I'm frightened," her voice ended at a high pitch.

The thought hit Tom that if Hendrix was the one planting the seeds of a serial killer amongst the Town Council, he probably, was also planting it among the men and woman reporting to him. More than likely, Hendrix was the one who needed to be watched.

"Lieutenant Braden," Janine's tone softened. She stood and walked between Tracie and Will's chairs. Placed both her palms flat on Tom's desk and leaned slightly forward. "Drew has an excellent background. He was well respected in the Criminal Justice System. Please, don't muddy his reputation with a scandal."

"A scandal?" Tom rolled his chair back and tilted his head. "So far, there is not a hint of a scandal in our murder investigation except that the Chief's wife had an affair with his Lieutenant."

A heavy silence fell over the room. An expression of sadness settled on Janine Williams's face and she seemed to recoil from his words. "The affair, as you call it, had ended, Lieutenant. Why does it have to be brought into the murder case? I assure you, I did not kill my husband, nor did Pat Hendrix."

"Ended?" Tracie repeated.

"Why?" Tom asked.

"It's better to be a grieving widow than a cheating wife," Will responded with a wry smile. His mouth settled in a thin line.

"I called it off days before Drew's murder," she retorted biting her lower lip. "And I didn't have any prior knowledge that he would be killed."

"But it gives both you and Hendrix a very, very strong motive," Tom said.

"Don't be ridiculous. It wasn't worth killing over."

"So, I'll ask again. Why did you break the affair off? And I'd like to know for how long was it going on?"

She swallowed hard, straightened up. "About a year. But I don't think I ever really mattered to Pat."

Janine turned and gave Will a snide look as she walked past his chair returning to hers and recrossing her legs.

But, before she could utter another word, Tom demanded, "How does Lawrence Ellridge fit into all of this?"

"He doesn't." Subtly, she started rubbing her neck just below her jawline. A pink indentation flared. "Drew and Lawrence were good friends that went way back. I don't even know if Pat and Lawrence knew each other. Though Pat was constantly interested in our lives. ALWAYS questioning! It's impossible remembering everything we said."

"What kind of questions? Personal?"

"Some. But also about Drew's work. At first, I thought I was using Pat as a sounding board for my frustrations, but then I realized every dinner, every drink Pat and I had together had a reason. And the reasons revolved around Drew and his job. Drew would come home not understanding how Pat always seemed a step ahead of him in the office, or on a case. I became suspicious. Didn't want this life. The affair became so cumbersome, it wasn't long before the excitement of it died."

The rubbing stopped. Her hand dropped into her lap. The bruise had turned a bright purple.

"What were you suspicious of?"

"I became convinced Pat wanted Drew's job. I think that was all he ever wanted. Not me. You'll see."

"Are you suggesting I am going to reward a suspect with the victim's job?"

Janine glanced around the room and smiled.

"She threw him under the bus," Will said dryly, watching Tracie escort Janine through the outer office where Vicky led her into the hallway and closed the door behind her.

"No love lost there." Tom stood hands on hips. "And I think we have a new suspect for our list."

"Are we being played?" Tracie asked returning.

"Definitely!" The two men responded.

CHAPTER TWENTY-FOUR

That night, during dinner, Tom rose from the table several times to prowl Kyra's kitchen. The first time, he wound up checking the slats in the knife rack as if he was doing a pre-op exam. The second time, he opened the door and stood on the threshold breathing in the sea air while contemplating the rear lawn and gate until Kyra patiently announced that desert was being served.

"Sorry," he said taking his seat and admiring the oversized piece of Tiramisu. "My favorite."

"That's what Barney mentioned. Serve Tiramisu and you'll do anything."

"Not quite anything." He chuckled, and then said, "It was a rough day and I'm afraid I'm pre-occupied."

"What happened?"

He told her about the meeting with Janine Williams and the trip to Boston. "I can't get rid of all the small details that are buzzing around in my head."

"They're not just about Ellridge and Mrs. Williams?"

"Most are, but there's much more going on. Our office finished the background check on Ellridge and the telephone company sent Tracie and Will data from the Chief's smart phone. I asked them to stop by with both reports. You don't mind, do you?"

"Of course, not. There is some dip left and maybe they would like something to drink. I can open a fresh bottle of wine and there's cold beer. We can go inside and talk," Kyra paused, a slight smile around her lips. "I heard that Matt included you in our little secret and you were not happy. I…."

"But he's happy," Tom interjected. "He drove in two runs, to-day." Tom caught her gaze and flashed a wide smile. "Thanks Kyra, I appreciate everything you did and Thank God it worked out fine, but…."

Before he could say another word, she reached up with one hand as if she was going to caress his face. But he met her half way, and instead interlocked their fingers pressing them against his heart.

"Tom, I wouldn't do anything to hurt Matt. Some of my best days were spent with him."

"I know, but… from now on, we have to be very careful about where we go and whom we are with until the killers are caught. Especially, when Matt is around."

"Killers! Plural?"

He heard the catch in her voice and softened his own. "We don't believe that the two murders are connected. I'll be back in a couple of minutes. There's something I have to check."

He jumped up again, re-opened the door and disappeared in the direction of the patio.

Kyra was setting up a plate of sandwiches for Tracie and Will when Tom came around the house from the opposite direction. Fast walking by the rear gate, he seemed to be taking in the orange and gold sunset. Then making a sudden turn, he came up the path.

But now, he had a knowing smile on his face and started speaking when he crossed the threshold. "The grounds merge into one huge piece of property that completely surrounds the house. A big house, three stories high, three wings and an attic. There's a four—car garage that's empty. To me, it seems that the entire downstairs of the building was rebuilt for the optimum beachfront view."

"True." Kyra nodded. "JE started to renovate as soon as he signed the mortgage. But what does that have to do with the Chief's murder?"

"No witnesses. No one saw anything. No one heard anything, yet dozens of people were wandering about. Williams seemed to have disappeared once he walked through the French doors and out to the patio. I didn't understand. But now, I get it. I saw that the gate, flight of stairs, most of the beach itself and the lower grounds are not visible unless you are on the house's upper floors.

From the first floor, only the lawns and front driveway can be seen."

"And of course, Nantucket Sound." She handed him a bottle of blush wine and a cold pack of beer. Picking up a bowl of cashew nuts, and the small tray of sandwiches, she headed for the living room. "And what did Ellridge have to say?" As she changed the subject, her shoulders stiffened.

She partially turned. Her eyes looked like two saucers.

He could see that her need to know about the lawyer was written across her face. She pressed her lips together trying to control her anxiety, waiting for him to respond.

"Several things. For one, Lawrence Ellridge claims he is devastated. Williams was his best friend since they met in college over thirty years ago. Yet, we already know that a couple of seasons could go by between phone calls. However, during the last few months, they were on the phone every day. Sometimes twice a day."

"What changed?" she snapped, swallowed hard.

He saw her chest heave. The muscles in her neck tightened. He felt that she anticipated the reason before the words were out of his mouth. "You were arriving from Miami and moving into the Cassel

Estate for several months. JE had put you in charge of building a five star resort on the Cape. From their conversations, these two men were extremely interested and very upset."

"I don't know what to say." Her tray of sandwiches shook. "Why? And what was their reason? You make it sound as if I might have been the intended victim and Megan was killed by mistake. Could this be why Williams insisted I was a person of interest? One way or the other, I was a target."

He stopped in his tracks. "That's the enigma. We don't know their plans, but we were told that whatever was discussed centered around you."

She stood as still as a statue and his heart went out to her.

She had arrived to do her job in good faith and it appeared that Ellridge and Williams had set out to stop her. Deep inside, she must have smothered a clue. Couldn't admit to what happened. He would not believe she lied to him. "Let me put this down. Then we'll talk." He hustled into the living room, placed the bottles on the coffee table. He returned to take the tray and bowl from her hands and brought them inside.

"I have to think, Tom," she said as he walked towards her. "Figure out what's going on, but first, let's get the rest of the things. They're still in the kitchen."

He followed her, tried grabbing her hand, but to his surprise, she pulled away and outpaced him.

In the kitchen, they gathered up glasses, small plates, a cork-screw, bottle opener and napkins, all of which she had left on the counter.

Deep in thought, she said nothing, licked her lips nervously. Just worked beside him putting everything in a large straw basket she had handed him.

When they returned to the living room, Tom settled in the corner of the sofa. He had reached for her, but she started pacing the room.

He couldn't allow this silence to go on. He couldn't handle problems this way. It gnawed its way into his belly. He rubbed his hand across the side of his jaw. "Kyra…."

As if reading his mind, she stopped pacing back and forth, walked toward him. "Ellridge told you all of this?" she asked incredulously.

"No. His secretary did."

"Marion Clark?"

"No. It turns out Ms. Clark is a partner and backs him on what ever he says. Sara Metcalf, the legal secretary, on the other hand, was quite open. The woman was unnerved when she heard that the Governor and the State of Massachusetts were investigating Ellridge and his staff about two murders. So, she answered all of Tracie's questions. Do you know Sara?"

"Never met her."

"There is something else. Ellridge insisted I was harassing him. As did Pat Hendrix!

But Ellridge said, he intends to address the issue with Mr. Cassel."

"Really?" Kyra's eyebrows arched.

"His words. Not mine. Is he that familiar with your boss?"

"Not to my knowledge. The first time they met was when Ellridge represented JE to buy this place. Someone had recommended him; and JE felt we could use a General Council in New England."

"That's only a couple of years ago. Ellridge must have gotten Mr. Cassel a great deal?"

"He did. JE wanted the view. That's what meant the most to him. The place was an estate sale and the family needed the money. Ellridge arranged for the seller to pay more than half of the renovations. JE had to pay less than half."

"JE probably figured he found a wheeler dealer in Lawrence Ellridge. A seller rarely pays that much to renovate a property, if the deal is already going through. That is, if he pays anything at all. We're talking about over one million dollars each. Right?"

"And some?" She sank into the opposite chair, eyes riveted on Tom. "After that, JE included him in several small deals. One was a land purchase in the northeast."

"How did that work out?"

"Okay."

"Just okay? What?" Tom leaned forward throwing his hands wide out.

"I was very surprised to find Ellridge would be working with me on this project."

"Did Ellridge ever mention Williams or Hendrix?"

"Absolutely not." Kyra shook her head. "I didn't even know if they knew each other until my party."

"What do you think about the story Janine Williams told us about her and Pat Hendrix?"

"At this point in time, I believe it's true. But to me, Williams looked and sounded tough. I wouldn't want to cross him. I think Mrs. Williams was a good match for her husband. And if he found out about the affair, I wonder if he told Ellridge? Those two, stone faced and mean spirited, they made quite a pair. I didn't trust either one and wouldn't put anything past them."

"Even murder?"

"Yes. Even murder."

The clap of the front bell resounded throughout the house. Tom saw Kyra's face whiten. She sucked in her breath.

"Don't worry," he said. "They're friends."

"Yours," she murmured. "And the State of Massachusetts. Not mine, they're the police."

CHAPTER TWENTY-FIVE

"Thanks for coming over," Tom said as all four trooped into the living room. "I know we had a long day, but I wanted to rehash everything while it was still fresh in our minds."

"Sandwiches! I know Kyra thought of this," Tracie said eyeing the table covered with food and drinks.

Kyra laughed.

Tom gave her I—told—you—so glance and she visibly relaxed.

Tracie put a half—stuffed turkey sandwich on a plate handed it to Will and took the same before sitting in the nearest chair to the coffee table.

The two newcomers ate quickly. Will poured a beer, Tracie a glass of wine.

Meanwhile, Tom munched on some nuts as he skimmed through the two reports Will had given him. By this time, he noticed they were all sitting around waiting for him to start.

Tracie put a small recorder on the table. "Tell me when you want it turned off."

Tom nodded and leaned forward in his chair; hands clasped between his knees. "There are two distinct problems that are stopping us from closing each case. In the first murder, we don't have any physical evidence that points to the killer. Nor do we have the weapon. We are guessing it has something to do with Kyra and JEC Industries' plans to build a resort on the Cape. Circumstantial evidence points to Ellridge and Chief Williams."

"A respected lawyer and a Chief of Police with an impeccable record who himself was stabbed to death." Will shook his head. "This evidence comes from benign telephone conversations overheard by a co-worker, Sara. We couldn't bring this case to trial, never mind convict. Now, if one of them had confessed on tape."

"Wishful thinking," Tracie remarked with a chuckle and picked up a second half of a sandwich. "They're delicious, Kyra. Thank you, so much. We were starved."

Kyra gave a weak smile, waited for the rest of the evidence they did not have that seemed to circumvent both her and her company.

"In the Chief's murder, Mrs. Williams points a strong finger at Hendrix, who does have a motive, but is that enough?" Tom paused, and then added. "The knife used to stab the Chief was from Kyra's kitchen and available to about half the town on Sunday, except for Hendrix, who wasn't invited."

"Not true," Kyra exclaimed, moving to the edge of her seat. "I did invite him, but he called, thanked me for the invitation, and apologized that he had to work Sunday to cover for Chief Williams."

"Interesting," Tracie said. "I didn't read that in any of the interviews or notes."

"I was never asked." Kyra looked from one to the other.

"Have you talked to Hendrix since then?" Tom leaned forward anger creased the corners of his eyes.

"It was the one and only time."

Jumping up, Tom started pacing the room. He was seething with fury. His voice loud and harsh, "When Lieutenant Hendrix arrived at the murder scene, he denied knowing about the party. Even denied knowing Kyra lived here, or that she was the hostess."

"If you didn't know the man, why did you invite him?" Will asked.

"I learned that he was a native of Whales Bay, very active in the community and friendly with Chief Williams and his wife. He was someone my company would want on their side, if a vote came up."

"A vote for what?"

"Zoning, real estate taxes. All sorts of propositions come into play when land changes owners and new buildings are erected."

The other three people in the room couldn't stop their eyes darting from one person to the other.

"This seems to enforce JEC Industries involvement with what happened," Will said.

"Or maybe Hendrix thought the party would be a great setting for a murder? So many people milling about?" Tracie murmured, shrugging a shoulder. "Do we know how Hendrix learned about his boss's stabbing?"

"I told him," Tom said. "I personally called Pat at the station. He left and met me at the crime scene within… less…than ten minutes. He had to have driven seventy—eighty miles per hour to get there so fast. Though, I am not positive where he was when he got the call. The Desk Sargent put me through, and I haven't had time to check.

Now—a—days, the phone providers are able to triangulate the calls. They can give us the exact areas where they originated. The Sargent could have connected me to Hendrix's mobile while Hendrix was standing on the patio watching the sunset and I wouldn't be the wiser."

Three pairs of eyes watched him, each with a different expression. He cleared his throat snapped out his words, "First thing in the morning, speak to Sargent Langford.

We're focusing on Hendrix, but discretely! We now know he is a natural born liar. Can turn positives into negatives. He has a strong motive and we have to verify where he was whenever he used his phone. Check his calls to the Chief, also to Mrs. Williams and Ellridge. We should learn if Hendrix and Ellridge were up to something. Then we will decide if the Lieutenant is a disgruntled lover, or a murderer? I don't want to tarnish his reputation unless we have some sort of physical evidence."

He saw Kyra's face, realized what he had just said hurt her, but he was not Williams.

He was not going to destroy another person, if he did not have too. He and his staff represented the Governor, owed it to Hendrix, as well as to the town to find the murderer, or eliminate innocent suspects. Other wise, the entire Cape area could suffer financially. He did not know what had motivated Chief Williams to act so indiscriminately toward Kyra unless it was Hendrix who prompted the Chief to smear her name for their own use.

"I'll check with the telephone providers," Tracie offered. Her expression telegraphed how she felt.

Kyra had stiffened, turned chalk white like she couldn't believe the words Tom had uttered. She seemed to bear the brunt of bad publicity.

"But why should she?" Tracie blurted aloud.

"I beg your pardon." Tom stared at her.

"I…" Tracie hesitated, cleared her throat. "Now is not the time."

"For what?" Tom demanded

"Never mind," she said. "While we were driving over, I skimmed through the telephone report. There were dozens of calls between the Chief and Pat Hendrix that could verify what Sara and Mrs. Williams said. I didn't have a chance to look up dates and times. Give me ten minutes."

Tom nodded a perplexed expression glazed his face. He rubbed the side of his jawline.

Tracie turned off the recorder, grabbed a highlighter from her purse and walked out.

Kyra heard the foyer chair move in the hall. She picked up the empty tray and some bottles bringing them into the kitchen. Her mind spun like a top. She had to protect herself especially after Tom's speech.

Why did he concentrate on the Chief's murder that had occurred only a couple of days ago and not on Megan's that was dragging her through the mud? But more important, his statement that he was worried about tarnishing Hendrix's reputation and yet, didn't give a damn about her's for almost two months.

All that mattered to Tom was his job to catch a killer. Any killer! Whatever seemed easier?

Tom glanced around the living room. An early spring drizzle had turned into a heavy rain and the downpour splattered on the windows. The darkness of ocean and sky pressed against the wall of glass.

He clapped his hands and a light went on.

Will stood and stretched, glanced at his smart phone, and read several e-mails.

Tom got up to look out across the horizon, but the sky was starless. There was nothing to be seen. He stopped at either corner to draw the blinds closed and realized Kyra sat like this most evenings vulnerable to occasional passing strangers and stalkers. Only the assailant who broke into her bedroom had introduced himself.

Perhaps, whoever was out to get Kyra, had left instructions to make it look like an accident and instead wound up in an altercation with Megan.

By the time, Kyra left the kitchen Tracie was practically jogging to the living room. A wide grin from ear to ear.

"What?" Kyra called, hurrying after the investigator.

"Hendrix was the one who made the last call to the Chief on Sunday afternoon," Tracie shouted. "He phoned about the time you saw the Chief turn purple, storm out of the party and disappear from the patio. It coincides within the realm of the Medical Examiner's time of death."

"First thing in the morning, call the phone company. Find out where Hendrix was when he placed the call?" Tom said pacing the room once again. "Finally something viable. Question Mrs. Nelson, Alex and every one who worked at the party. Confirm if Pat Hendrix was seen on Sunday around the kitchen area and the house?"

"Or the mud room?" Kyra interjected. "Someone tried on several occasions to get into the rear of the house. Maybe he was tampering with the lock on Sunday."

"Why didn't you tell me?" Tom whirled about.

"At the time, I didn't think it would serve any purpose." Kyra shrugged. "You were already preoccupied with so much on your plate."

Silence settled on their shoulders.

Tracie added softly. "There could have been finger prints, foot prints, tracks from car tires. It happened before the party. Right?"

"Yes. I'm sorry, I didn't think of that, but I'm not a cop."

"That's why, we ask everyone to recall every little thing," Tracie said. "We put the facts together and they tell a story."

"I understand, but I have my own job to do. I can't think of every-one else's."

Tracie licked her lips, pursed her mouth. "Kyra, you have to help us. Megan's case is dragging out, getting colder. If we are correct about Ellridge and the Chief, why were they so upset that you were coming to the Cape, and why were they trying to pin her murder on you? There has to be something you're not telling us."

"There's nothing to tell," Kyra glared at Tracie. "You sound like Tom."

"Is there something you forgot, or don't think is important like the footsteps or the tires?" Tracie continued, ignoring Kyra's remarks.

"That's been Tom's theory. No facts. Just wild accusations."

"Kyra!" Tom took a long breath. "There is something we learned today, that we thought would upset you, but now I believe you should know. Ellridge was a criminal lawyer before he specialized in real estate?"

"So?" Kyra's eyes flashed from Tracie to Tom.

"He ran with a tough crowd. It also means Ellridge has the knowledge and connections to hire a hit man," Tom explained.

"You're just supposing."

"True, and we are still not sure, if and why he wanted you dead?" Will added.

"You don't know if Ellridge or anyone else did?" Kyra stood. Nausea moved from inside her chest up into her throat.

"That's the problem. We don't know. If we did, we could proceed in the right direction," Tom snapped.

Kyra riveted her eyes to his. Wondered if she would ever forgive him. The evening had torn her apart. "If Ellridge changed careers more than several years ago it happened before he worked for my company and before I knew him." She hesitated a moment.

"But there is something, I thought of. It's nonsense, like most everything else. When I landed in Boston and was loading my luggage into the rental car at Logan Airport, someone tried to run me down. I thought it was a rotten driver, but if you're fishing around for suspects? That's as good as I can give you."

"Before you even arrived on the Cape?" Tom pressed. No surprise or questions on his face, just a cold blankness.

Kyra nodded.

"Then that means..."

"We're back to the Chief and Ellridge," Will mumbled.

"I'm exhausted. I'd like to lock up now." Kyra turned and gave a half smile. "You know there is no one thing that defines my job description. There are different answers, curves and reasons I have to come up with each day. Not one definition per motive that the police have."

"Perhaps..." Tom reached out a hand. "I can lock up for you."

"It's not necessary and I have some calls to make." Kyra walked into the foyer, followed by Tracie who carried the rest of the dirty dishes.

She saw Tom and Will standing near the sofa, mumbling.

Tracie stopped by her side. "Kyra, I wouldn't mind staying over. I feel we need some girl talk. Tom cares...."

"I'm too old for that. And I have to phone my boss."

A half hour later pulling her bedroom drapes closed, Kyra recalled what they all forgot to ask.

How did she learn all the background information on Hendrix?

CHAPTER TWENTY-SIX

K yra immediately rang JE who picked up the phone exhaling deeply.

His drowsy voice complained, "Must you always call on the nights I retire early?"

"I only call when it's important." She heard the catch in her throat. Felt that he heard it, too.

"Kyrita, what happened?" He demanded.

She could hear the movement of his body against the linen. He had sat up quickly. There was a murmur of a woman's voice. No wonder he was annoyed. But she was even more annoyed. Her evening had turned into a disaster. "The police are pointing at Lieutenant Hendrix as Chief Williams' murderer."

"Thank God! Great news. This killing will not be blamed on JEC or our employees."

"No." she murmured. Anyway, there was only one employee they had ever blamed—ME.

"And the dead red headed woman?"

"They're still working on the case."

"Is that why you are so upset, Kyrita?"

She took a long breath. No use playing the denial game. "Absolutely. But it should be quieter now and I can get some work done. Perhaps, it would be a good time to begin further negotiations for the Dickerson property?"

"Don't you think you should wait until you are cleared of the woman's murder? Opponents can start a smear campaign."

"I've never been officially accused. Even the newspapers have forgotten about me?" Her stomach rolled over. Kyra sank to the bed. The Chief had perpetuated his own smear campaign. Did he do it at Ellridge's request?

Ellridge, who also whispered into JE's ear, JE who never forgot anything?

Swallowing the bile rising up into her throat, Kyra said, "Something new was also discussed tonight."

"What?"

"If you were aware that Ellridge used to be a criminal lawyer?"

"Doesn't sound familiar. You know me, unless something is specifically brought to my attention, I ignore it. There is a limit to how much I can remember. If you recall, Kyrita, we used him to buy the Summer Place. He was not one of us. Not a true business executive. When we needed a local lawyer for the Cape Resort, we threw him a bone."

"So, we did, JE. So, we did. It's exactly what I said."

"Why were you asked?"

"Lieutenant Braden believes Ellridge was responsible for hiring the hit man who killed Megan McDermott by mistake."

"McDermott? I thought her name was Polk."

"That was her maiden name. McDermott was her married name."

"She was the Zoning Commissioner's wife?"

"Yes."

"And why would Ellridge do such a stupid thing?"

"They say to kill me. Get my job. Perhaps, I should terminate Ellridge?"

"He reports to you, Kyrita. Tell him anything you wish. Do anything you wish. As I've always said, we are business people. Maybe, you've been hanging around too long with police and murderers. Perhaps, it's time you came home?" He heaved a big sigh.

"JE, did you betray me? Promise Ellridge my job, if and when you got rid of me?"

"How can you even think of such a thing?" He gave a sudden laugh.

It felt like pinpricks on her skin.

"You will have to look elsewhere for the betrayer. I could never hurt you. I lost one woman that still tears me apart. I cannot lose another. Besides Kyrita, Criminal lawyers are not killers. They just defend them."

"But they also have the connections to hire them."

"I have Alesandro who is always ready to take your place. Why do I need a stranger?"

Kyra heard the ping of an incoming call while she was speaking to JE, but ignored it. Finally, she said goodnight and hung up. She stretched, lay down, and closed her eyes.

The phone rang again. Caller ID announced Tom's name. "Be strong," she whispered in the stillness of her bedroom. "You have to answer. If you don't, he's liable to send a patrol car to check."

She picked up on the fourth ring.

"I was about to drive over," Tom said.

"It's late and I'm tired. It was a rough night."

"I'm sorry, Kyra for what happened this evening. The case continues and you still drop new information on me."

"I can't have this conversation now."

"When then?"

"I'll drop in at the station tomorrow." She felt sad, felt tears pooling in her eyes. She really cared for this man, but now felt there was no way for them to continue.

"How about if I stop off in the morning with breakfast?"

"Please don't."

"This is awkward. I feel you are deliberately…"

"Tom, let's cool it for a while. Catch your murderers. I'm behind schedule and owe it to JE to bring the best deal possible to the table. I realize I'm not cut out to be with a cop, especially one who lives at the other end of the coastline."

"I can't believe you're saying this. Millions of people work and have healthy relationships, Kyra. Even cops."

"Most of them don't live over fifteen hundred miles apart. I have no other options. I'm worried sick over my job. I put in years working my way to the top and now I feel everything is about to fall down. This was meant to be a short, happy relationship."

"Not to me."

"I'm sorry, Tom." As her tears flowed down her cheeks, Kyra hung up the receiver.

⚒ ⚒

Niomi Cooper said she was renting her father's Cape Cod beach house one block from Nantucket Sound. The next morning, Kyra followed her directions and found the gray-shingled bungalow in less than ten minutes.

Niomi had promised a continental breakfast and the latest gossip.

"I had no idea, you lived so close," Kyra said.

"My dad stopped renting out the place when I decided to come home. It's worked out pretty good. Most mornings, I drive into town, stop at the courthouse to find out what happened during the prior twenty-four hours, and then visit his newspaper. I go through the articles and chat with the reporters. Between court and the newspaper,

I pick up a case or two. Sometimes I don't. But I find, more and more clients are phoning the office or just walking in. I pay my own way, and I love living close to the water."

"Then it's true what I heard, that you are building your own general practice."

"Definitely trying." Niomi shrugged, looked across at Kyra as she placed a plate of home baked cranberry muffins in the center of the table. "I was surprised when you called last night. I thought JEC Industries traveled with their own private group of lawyers."

"Only when there is a contract to sign," Kyra smiled. "If you don't mind, Niomi, can you tell me about your experience?"

"Of course. I clerked for a judge in Boston. Then worked for a mid-size firm for about a year. Decent salary, worked most weekends, hardly any social life. They handled different types of cases and took whichever ones came their way. It was great experience. Then I started seeing someone I knew from school, but he wanted to move to a warmer climate and I didn't.

After a while, I became lonely, somewhat bored, and I decided to come home. Figured I'd give it a year. If it worked, I'd try for another year, and so on. Kept going. It's almost three years now and I took over the cottage." Niomi flourished a hand around the room.

"And..."

"I'm my own boss. Have time to see my family and friends. Made some new ones. I do some pro bono work that at times makes me feel real good, and I don't have to answer to anyone I don't respect. I'm not looking to set the world on fire. Just want to be able to support myself and be interested in the work I'm doing."

Kyra focused on Niomi's face as if she was studying a textbook. "I want to be clear about one thing. You'll be working for me, not JEC Industries. I don't want you to get the wrong idea."

"I won't. And I already changed my plans for the week. There is nothing that I can't work on simultaneously. I haven't been so excited since I graduated law school."

Kyra grinned. "Now let's discuss the Zoning Commissioner, his wife and his girlfriend."

"Charlotte Ellis," Niomi added.

CHAPTER TWENTY-SEVEN

*H*e had been given a key. Zippered it into his sleeve pocket, that and the security code he had memorized. Tomorrow, the money would be in his account. He was set to go.

By the time he arrived in Whales Bay, the drizzle that followed him down the coastline had turned into a heavy downpour.

The water ran over his hood and down his slicker. He could barely see as he tied the boat to the dock. He sloshed his way along the beach, up the wooden stairs and across the rain swept lawn, the sky black, and the weather dank.

He un-zippered his sleeve, grabbed the key, and unlocked the rear door. Closing it behind him, he punched in the code.

The house was dark and silent. He could hardly make out the back stairs to his right.

Slowly, he inched his way to the second floor and walked down the hall. Her door was ajar an inch or so. He picked up speed as he entered the room and pulled the knife from his cargo pants pocket. He made a running lunge toward the mussed bed and brought the blade down with a slashing motion.

But instead of skin, bones and blood, he saw the knife rip through a pillow, and as the feathers flew, he cursed aloud, "Damn! Damn!"

The bed was empty.

He whirled about.

A night bulb blinked from inside the bathroom. Something fluttered and he hustled forward. The bitch was hiding beyond the shower door.

He didn't know what he had seen, but he found this room empty, too.

"I have to get out of here," he hissed turning in a circle. "I'm taking too long. She can walk in with someone at any moment. I have to return, but when."

No more mistakes, he'd been told, or there would be no money.

His boss had been right. "Ms. Stevens, you're one lucky bitch," he shouted feeling his face flush red and hot.

He ran back into the hallway, punching the doorjamb on his way out, and fled down the stairs. He bolted through the rear door and left it swinging behind him. Let them wonder who had been there.

No one was to be seen or heard.

Where was she?

The garden door squeaked as it swung in slow motion from the rain. Someone's footsteps were coming around the building, too heavy and too loud to be Ms. Stevens.

⊷ ⊶

"Who's there?" Tom shouted hearing what sounded like a door repeatedly opening and closing and footsteps sloshing through the grass and mud.

He came around the corner pulling his gun from the oversized pocket in his slicker and called out, "Police! Stop!"

Several yards ahead of him, someone was running toward the rear gate and wooden steps. "Police! Stop."

Tom shot his gun in the air as a warning. Reaching the gate, he saw no sign of the intruder.

Quickly, he returned the gun to his pocket and called the station from his shoulder phone giving them a few seconds of a synopsis.

When he stepped out on the landing, he saw a figure run north-west along the beach and disappear. He shouted again, "Police, Stop!" Then grabbed the night scope from his pocket attached it to the .357-caliber gun and flicked the blue nightlight on.

Pointing the gun straight out, he looked through the scope and saw the running man. "Police! Stop!" Tom shouted as loud as he could. "The Perp is headed to the dock," Tom yelled into his phone, and pulled the trigger.

The man fell to one leg. "Wounded the S.O.B. I'm going back to the house to see if Stevens is okay. The guy can't go far dragging one bleeding leg. Send an ambulance and EMTS. Tom ran back to the rear door and up the stairs, calling, "Kyra, Kyra."

No answer. He pushed open her bedroom door. "Kyra."

The room was empty.

A few feathers flew above her bed.

Her bathroom was empty.

There were only clothes and whatever else belonged in a double closet.

As he went through the house, he opened doors and called her name. She didn't answer or come forward.

His heart sank.

He ran down the back stairs and out to the rear gate still screech-ing in the cold rain. He headed up the beach through the icy foam that dragged rivulets of sand back into the water. Once again, he raised the gun and peered through the scope. Nothing.

Could the intruder have faked the wound? He didn't know, but he had to keep going.

Finally, he saw what could be blood mixing with the ocean foam, the sand and the rain. And knew he had definitely hit the guy.

He fast walked, moving his scope sideways from left to right and right to left. And just as the beach turned towards the Sullivan Compound, Tom saw the matted sea grass and the pools of rainwater.

He pointed his gun, walked a few steps closer and shouted, "Police! Stop, or I'll shoot."

To his surprise, the intruder shot first.

Tom squeezed the trigger and the man dropped.

CHAPTER TWENTY-EIGHT

Floodlights lit up the beach and the surrounding areas. Police, firemen, ambulances and EMTS were milling about. A Coast Guard Cutter was angling off shore. The rain had stopped. A raw wind had taken its place and swept through their clothes and bodies.

"No sign of her yet," Tom said to Barney who had just arrived, hands clenched in his pockets. Both there faces raw and red, Tom's eyes bleary and bloodshot. "The first time I shot someone and killed him. Usually, when I aim it's to bring the suspect down. This time, I had no choice."

"He's a murderer. Shot at you first. He didn't want to be caught."

"I thought he was a knife man, had no idea he carried a gun."

"Tom, you..."

"It's Kyra's phone ring." Tom grabbed his cell shouting into it. "Where are you? Are you okay?"

"Yes," she said, her voice husky with sleep. "I just heard."

"How?"

"One of Bryant Cooper's reporters called and told him. Bryant phoned Niomi."

"And?"

"I had stayed at her place for the night. We were going to Boston the first thing in the morning. It just seemed easier to leave together. Plus, we had a lot to discuss."

"I didn't realize you were that friendly. You must have known I would go crazy, worrying. I don't understand why you didn't call and tell us you were staying at Niomi's. I searched the house and grounds. I didn't know if you were dead or alive. The police are still going over the entire area."

"I'm so sorry, Tom. I thought we were over."

"I can't turn my emotions on and off, Kyra. I thought you would realize that. I'm sending a car to pick you up."

"Wait! I have an appointment…"

"Doesn't matter. You can reschedule. A man is dead. I need you to identify, if he is the assassin who broke into your bedroom."

He pressed END, waved to Officer Pirro, and met him half way issuing instructions. Then turned to Barney. "Just two days and already Kyra and I are in separate places."

Kyra pulled on jeans, sneakers and a hooded sweatshirt. She had caught her hair back in a ponytail and was standing outside the front door when Officer Pirro turned into the driveway.

Niomi ran out and handed Kyra a scarf. "It'll be brutal out there. If you need me, call."

"It won't be necessary, but thanks anyway." Kyra climbed into the back seat of the patrol car.

A thousand thoughts zipped through her mind. She had been lucky tonight. Strange how things happened!

"I'm really glad you're okay, Ms. Stevens. All of us were worried."

To Tom, Kyra looked like the most wonderful thing he ever saw when she got out of the police car. He wanted to run and put his arms about her, but thought better of it.

Then to his surprise, she ran toward him, slid on the mud and landed up against his body. He caught her with his hands, held tight, and she reached up with one of hers, gently patting the side of his face. "Are you okay?"

He nodded, placed her arm through his, and carefully led her around the puddles of water and mud to a small group of men standing in the middle of a crowd of investigators.

"Only say what you're sure of," Tom said in a low tone.

The crowd stepped aside to let them through and she looked down, grimaced and turned away. She looked down a second time and her eyes roved along the body.

She felt that everyone was focusing on her while she focused on the dead man. She started to shake jammed her hands into her pockets and swallowed hard, not wanting to throw up in front of them.

Tom squeezed her arm. Through the linings of their clothes, he pressed their hands together and suddenly she felt safe, her insides calm.

"The eyes and nose definitely those of the man who broke into my room. He's about the same built and size. He—he looks as if he is wearing the same pants. I can't swear to the rest of his face. He wore a fake beard and mustache when he attacked me."

She looked at Tom.

Rage started twisting in her stomach and in her chest. She knew it reflected on her face.

JE was right. She was a business executive. Worked hard. So, why did someone cause such an upheaval in her life? Trying to destroy her. Why?

She leaned against Tom. "Do you know who he is?"

"We ran his fingerprints through IAFIS and should have the answer in a few hours."

———✦⁛✦———

Kyra had returned to Niomi's house, slept a couple of hours and showered before she drove into town. The sky had cleared and the sun was rising over the horizon. She watched it, a golden orange color, as she parked her car and walked into the Police Station. She should be walking into a Board Room for a meeting, or lying on a beach with a man she loved, not protecting herself from fear and harm.

"Did you find out who hired him?" Kyra asked as she sat in Tom's office sipping her second cup of hot coffee.

"No, but in his pocket, we found his key to your rear door along with the security code. Who else had copies?"

She shook her head, couldn't stop her nerves from tingling. "JE gave me his keys, but outside of the company's Personnel Department in Miami, he might have had another set. Though I doubt it. And he certainly didn't bother memorizing a security code, never mind writing it down."

"Why do you say that?"

"He doesn't bother with small details. That's why he has me. JE had nothing to do with hiring a hit man. He might lie to me, but he would never have betrayed me. If he didn't want me around, he'd just say good-bye. He always has a back up. You should go on to other possibilities."

"Like who?"

Their eyes met. Right now, this was not how she wanted things to go. But she was the one who had started this conversation.

"We found evidence," Tom continued, "that the assassin was in your bedroom last night, slashed your pillow, searched your bathroom and closets. His knife and your slashed pillow look like they matched the size and blade of the murder weapon used to kill Megan. It'll take a couple of days—to—a—week to identify if it is the same one."

"Talk to Lawrence Ellridge. I believe he knows who the killer is."

"We've spoken to him once and got no place. We need some physical evidence. Don't forget he's a Criminal Attorney. Knows his rights."

"Yesterday, I called Ellridge and set up an appointment for today. Said I was driving to Boston this morning. I planned on firing him. It's the reason I hired Niomi. I wanted a lawyer as a witness. I didn't want Ellridge to make up lies afterwards and shift my words around. He is quite good at that. When I phoned he could have realized what I intended and sent the hit man for one last attempt."

"Do you have cause?"

"A list. For starters, he told lies about important matters to the CEO, withheld information, and was pocketing a personal commission."

"He skimmed money off the top?"

"That he did."

"Why didn't you tell us when Tracie and Will were pressuring you? When I kept asking."

"I felt it was a company problem. We didn't need a scandal mudding the waters. People don't kill each other over internal personal disagreements."

"This person is trying very hard to do so," Tom mumbled. A quick shadow of annoyance slid over his face. He tapped his fingers in a staccato beat on the desk. "And his relationship with Williams?"

"They were working together on something. I'm not sure what. But Ellridge did have a key and the security code from the time he was buying the estate. JE has no idea what happened to either one after the sale. Though he arranged to have both changed. As the attorney on record, Ellridge must have manipulated to get his own copies. JE also reminded me that Ellridge and Williams both grew up in Boston and on the Cape. They lived in and knew the area all their lives. I feel like a sitting duck." Her eyes filled with tears. She blinked, trying to hold them back. "Which reminds me, what happened with Hendrix?"

"He's under arrest. Insists he is innocent and hired a criminal lawyer to defend him."

"Who?"

"A guy recommended by the Boston Police Union. Has an excellent reputation."

She nodded her head and stood. Concentrated on speaking in a modulated tone. "I'd like to go home, Tom. Are your men finished in the house?"

"I'll check," Tom gave her a quick glance, reached for his phone. "You can always come home with me. My family is worried. They'll take good care of you."

"I need a little breathing space." She managed to get the words out, still torn, not knowing what to do.

"Will we be all right?" He put a hand over hers.

"It's not that simple." She leaned over and brushed her lips across his cheek. "I wanted to call yesterday, but I was very hurt from what was said the night before. And I found it hard to believe that someone of Ellridge's stature could have hired a man to slit my throat." She choked on the words, gagged. "Please, I want to go home."

He punched in several numbers. "Is the house clear?" He nodded his head in her direction. "Ms. Stevens will be there, shortly. Stop anyone who goes up the driveway, or the beach stairs."

⚊⚊⚊

A patrol car was parked diagonally at the top of her driveway. The police were still on guard. She clicked open the car door, got out, waved and went into the house.

She flipped through the mail, shredded most of it, filed the rest in the desk and picked up her laptop.

Walking upstairs, all she could think about was her life, Tom, and her plans for the future. All of which, had changed in a day.

"Good Morning, Ms. Stevens. I understand you had an exciting night. I think your day will top it." Lawrence Ellridge came from behind the bedroom door, dressed in jeans, work boots and work gloves, a gun in his hand.

Kyra screamed. Stood shocked still.

"I doubt if any one heard you. This place is built like a fortress." He took a step closer. "But if I was you..."

With all her force, she swung the computer upwards right between his legs. His gun dropped, his knees buckled and he grunted, "God Damn Bitch. You're going to be dead in five minutes."

She ran into the hallway and toward the back stairs. All the time thinking, maybe he had the key, but maybe he didn't know where the rear staircase was. Besides which, she could hear him moan. Probably, bent over, too.

She slammed the hall door behind her, flew down the stairs and out the garden door. The alarm went off.

And she started screaming.

A patrol officer jumped over the gate, running in her direction. "He's in the house," she shouted.

"Who?"

"Lawrence Ellridge, with a gun. Call the Lieutenant."

"Stay on the beach," he shouted.

She unlocked the gate ran down half a flight, and then jumped to the sand. She started running, kept close to the sea wall, but was having trouble catching her breath. She made it to the boulders that jutted out into the foam and sank to the ground, panting.

She squeezed into the shadows up against the wall and for the briefest of seconds closed her eyes.

Someone was thrashing through the brush, but she couldn't run any more. She pressed tighter against the wall, tried holding her breath, but a man's steps sounded closer.

And she realized whoever it was wouldn't see her unless he jumped down into the sand. From the distance, she could hear men shouting. She needed only three or four minutes for the police to reach them.

Just three or four minutes that now seemed like a lifetime.

Slowly, she dragged over the sand towards her a piece of driftwood from last night's storm and as she brought it closer grabbed it in two hands like a bat.

Whoever was thrashing about moved closer. She raised her eyes. Saw the tips of the work boots, the bottom of his jeans. It was Ellridge. She burrowed into the wall.

He was leaning down, and jumped, as she stood, swinging her bat and whacked him full force above the ankles.

"Bitch," he screamed landing in the sand and almost knocking her down.

She hit him again with the driftwood. He tried to turn and roll away. She saw the gun half hidden in his jean pocket.

Yanking it out, Kyra pointed it in his bloody face. "Don't move, or I'll shoot the damn thing into your lying mouth."

"No you won't," he hissed. "It's not in your DNA. You attacked me and I'm the company lawyer."

"You were never the company lawyer. What are you talking about? Why were you trying to kill me?"

"It was the easiest way to get rid of you and take your job."

"My job?" She bent down on her haunches. "And Williams?"

"I didn't kill Williams. I promised him head of security at JEC, if he helped tarnish your reputation."

"All of this was about a job?"

"No." He laughed. "It was prestige and money, a great deal of money. You're finished. The publicity and notoriety will work for me, not you."

"But not according to JE. I was going to Boston to fire you. It's over."

But in that instance, Ellridge rolled back, raised his head and hand and punched her in the jaw.

Her finger automatically pulled the trigger and she plopped frozen on the ground. Drops of his blood splattered on her.

It seemed like hours, but it was only a few minutes before Tom lifted and pressed her to his chest. Gently, he wiped the blood from her face.

Someone pried her finger open and took the gun from her hand.

"It was all about two jobs," Kyra sobbed.

EPILOGUE

The sun was slowly sliding into the sea. The warm August breeze cooled off the last dozen or so people lingering on the beach. A few boys and girls playful stomped through the frothy foam lining the water's edge.

"I found one. I found one," Matt shouted as he ran from the water towards Kyra holding a Conch straight out in his two hands.

Tom followed, laughing. "We can pack up and go home now," he said. "Our mission is complete. Matt, if we're having it for dinner. Fine. Put it in the pail. If not, throw it back into the sea."

"I don't think I can eat it, Dad."

"Okay, then. Throw it back."

Kyra put down her Kindle and jumped up to examine the shellfish. "Wait. Let me have a look. Nah. I couldn't eat it, either," she said wrinkling her nose.

A couple of boys Kyra and Tom had invited for the day hurried over to share Matt's excitement.

"Are you and Matt in the same class at school this term?" Kyra asked.

"Yes," Pete nodded. "Also, we're on the same bus."

"Great," Kyra said with a smile helping Tom to shake out the blanket.

"JE called earlier," she murmured.

Tom arched an eyebrow. "What did he want?"

"He was approached about his plans for the Whales Bay resort and condominiums."

"And?"

"He told them if his Ex-Vice President is interested than he will be."

"How do you feel about it?"

"It's a big job. Big money. He wants me to supervise the entire construction, including the project manager."

"Why? It's not what you usually did."

"Right now, I'm the only one he trusts. He says Ellridge taught him a lesson and he should have listened to me sooner. But that doesn't change things. There's all the time that I would have to be involved. And at this point, I don't want to return to the rat race."

"Did you tell him about your plans with Niomi?"

"I just said I'm starting my own company. Dealing with business problems involving legal, accounting, and theft. It will take a while to get under way and I am not ready to make another commitment. But I made a new home with you and Matt and I sold my Florida condo."

She glanced at her watch. "I think there's time for a ride through the dunes. Don't you?" She looked up at Tom put her hand in his. "I'm content for now," Kyra said with a smile. "I don't have to say or do anything else."

THE END

www.ingramcontent.com/pod-product-compliance
Lightning Source LLC
Chambersburg PA
CBHW071147170626
46809CB00002B/804